Praise for Lana Citron

Sucker

'*Sucker* is remarkable for the emergence of a brave new prose stylist . . . [Citron's] boldness makes for an invigorating read' *Independent*

'*Sucker* stands out from other urban twenty-something novels for its genuinely witty and original writing' *Literary Review*

'Lively and absorbing . . . Citron's recording eye rarely misses a thing. This novel is a wicked but affectionate satire' *Daily Telegraph*

'Citron has a very sharp eye for the rules and manipulations of the sex war. She's idiosyncratic, clever and, like her name, full of zest' *Observer*

'Romance for anti-romantics . . . Citron's straight-talking style and uncompromising approach to male/female relationships is the ideal antidote if you're schmaltzed up to the eyeballs' *Cosmopolitan*

Spilt Milk

'The overall effect is something like Dr Dre meeting James Joyce at a party thrown by Jackie Collins. This is dangerous prose . . . An exhilarating read' *Scarlett Thomas*

'With an attitude worthy of Eminem's generation . . . Citron retains her distinctive voice: sassy, quirky – undeniably infectious' *Literary Review*

'If you've had enough of fluffy romance novels, you'll love this. Totally engrossing' *Heat*

'A cracking love story . . . A superb read if you like your books offbeat' *Glamour*

GW00501481

Lana Citron is the author of *Sucker* and *Spilt Milk*. Born in Dublin, she now lives in London.

LANA CITRON

TRANSIT

Scribner

First published in Great Britain by Scribner, 2002
This edition published by Scribner, 2003
An imprint of Simon & Schuster UK Ltd
A Viacom Company

Copyright © Lana Citron, 2002

This book is copyright under the Berne Convention
No reproduction without permission
® and © 1997 Simon & Schuster Inc. All rights reserved

'I Have a Dream' reprinted by permission of Bocu Music Ltd,
1 Wyndham Yards London, W1H 2QF. Composers:
Benny Andersson/Bjorn Ulvaeus. 'Stuck in the Middle With You' used by
permission of Baby Bun Music Ltd and Universal Music.

Scribner and design are trademarks of Macmillan Library Reference USA, Inc.,
used under licence by Simon & Schuster, the publisher of this work.

The right of Lana Citron to be identified as author of this work has been asserted
by her in accordance with sections 77 and 78 of the Copyright, Designs and
Patents Act, 1988.

1 3 5 7 9 10 8 6 4 2

Simon & Schuster UK Ltd
Africa House
64–78 Kingsway
London WC2B 6AH

Simon & Schuster Australia
Sydney

www.simonsays.co.uk

A CIP catalogue record for this book is available from the British Library

ISBN 0-7432-2105-2

The publishers have made every reasonable effort to trace the copyright
holders of all material contained in this book. Where it has not been possible
to trace copyright holders, the publishers will be happy to credit them in all
future editions.

Typeset by M Rules
Printed and bound in Great Britain by Cox & Wyman Ltd, Reading, Berks

To ....
(Your name here)

Gloria in Excelsis

She had it coming to her.

'Look, I'm not making excuses for my behaviour ...
Angel? Angel?' I'm sat in a seedy caff beside Angel.

'Are you listening to me?'

'What?'

'Sal. It was for her own good.'

I stare across at Angel, awaiting her response as she sits,
slurping weak tea through a straw 'cause her face is so beat up
and swollen. One final suck, then she rests the straw on her
puffed-up lower lip and slurs,

'So Ed. You're claiming it was what – a mercy killing?'

'That's precisely what it was.'

Stupid, sad, fucked-up Sal got exactly what she deserved.

'Yeah, sometimes you got to be cruel to be kind.'

Gloria's Coffee Cabin, down a dead-end street, off of a back
alley, deep in the wastelands of this vast city. London,
two a.m., 14th February, year 2000 and two. Eerie after hours
and it wasn't the type of place you'd stumble upon. Not my
usual territory; we were beyond the beaten track. It stood on
the side of the road like a permanent shed painted evergreen
and owing its existence to black cabbies.

It had taken us an age to find. Thanks be, we had and in

we went, tripping over the hard-bristled 'Home Sweet Home' mat. A hot blower hung right above the door of the caff, misleading the punter with a blast of heat lasting all of three feet. Bar us there was only herself, Gloria, sat slouched over, flicking through celebrity pictures in an out of date gossip magazine. A small transistor radio at her side played trashy, tinny music, love songs for the heavy hearted to drift off on.

Sal's kind of music, catchy chorus with crappy sentiments.

Our arrival caused Gloria to raise her sharply arched eyebrows, her eyes pinched and fixed on us.

I get this a lot now, due in essence to the state of Angel. I offered an explanation.

'I'm meeting Fischer. The Russian guy.'

'Oh.' She recognized the name.

Gloria wasn't happy. Strictly speaking her gaff was restricted to trade only and not open to members of the public. She scrunched her mouth into a lopsided grimace as if to say 'I'll have words with Fischer later', which then slipped into a look of distaste.

'You okay?' She addressed this to Angel, staring first at her beat-up face, then at me, like I could have done it and before you ask, I didn't.

'It looks worse than it is.'

Gloria handed me a laminated menu.

Angel asked for a cup of tea and a straw.

We sat down the back, facing the mirror, away from Gloria's gaze.

'I had to get rid of Sal.'

'Ed, you already told me.'

'Well sweet Angel, I'm telling you again.'

'The truth Ed?'

'Maybe.' And I said to her, 'Angel, you got to ask the right questions, otherwise we're just going round in circles.'

We'd been going round in circles. It had taken us forever to find this place. I was cursing Fischer – he'd left directions scrawled on the back of an Indian take-away menu. They'd seemed pretty straightforward; guess that's appearances for you.

Cold and soaked through, we had spent the past hour stumbling round like blind idiots. Angel at my side, the rain running down the back of my neck, beneath my t-shirt and my trainers not as waterproof as they claimed to be. A constant downpour, heavy, bouncing off the pavement, the wet film reflecting colours of shop signs and passing headlights. On a night like this, you'd only go out if you really had to. We really had to and I was stressing about the ten grand in my back pack. I damned Fischer, his crappy directions and for making us meet him the arse end of nowhere. The thought double crossed my mind, he may have concocted a counter plan to my own, that he was about to stitch us up, but I recalled the way he'd looked at Angel when he was fixing her up and how he had flashed that sparkling, gold-toothed grin at her. Besides he'd no idea I was actually going to carry the money on me. We'd hovered around the vicinity waiting for a clue and then a cab swung out of a side-street.

An hour before Angel had dismissed the shed straight out, mistaking the place for a builders' hut. I should have trusted my own instinct. There you go and it put me in a real shitty mood. Huddled up beneath the portico of a derelict building, taking shelter from the rain, I'd spun around,

'Jesus Angel, if it wasn't for you, we'd be dry.'

She shouted back at me, 'And if it wasn't for you Ed, I'd be dead.'

See, I'm not totally bad.

So in the pair of us had ventured, pushing the door open to reveal a cramped space with dirty white walls and a large mirror hung at the far end. Caravan benches with screwed-down tables semi-circled one half of the room, while the other half was neatly partitioned by a small makeshift counter, behind which sat Gloria.

Believe me, I had good reason to kill Sal. The three principal ones being Sal, Rob and Frank.

Angel and I glance down the menu. Angel . . . I mean it's such a ridiculous name. She agrees. 'Angel' is a pseudo and she's keeping schtum in case of recognition. We're in the middle of a game where she's set to play hooker, right, left, and her two black eyes stare back at me, her gormless smile missing one front tooth.

I've always had a load of questions I wanted to ask a prostitute, mainly what it's like to have dick inside of you for hours on end, every day, and get paid for it. And I wonder can you really tell by looking at a man's hands?

Angel sniggers, well she tries, pointing to my own.

Gloria shouts from behind the counter,

'Are you ready to order?'

My head feels fit to burst.

'Change the station. The music, it's getting to me.'

Dumb tunes, dum di dum, dum dum.

'Ed, shut up,' mutters Angel.

The airwaves are flooded with one of Sal's favourite songs. *Tra la la my heart is broke, I'd give you my soul to walk all over me.* Sal had such crap taste in music.

'I'll have the meatballs. Are they organic?'

'What's that?' snaps Gloria.

It's a joke. 'I think I'll have the meatballs.'

Angel wants the meatballs too, as long as I mush them up into tiny bits for her and she wonders if they come with rice or potatoes. Gloria throws up her eyes, hoping we won't get difficult. My forehead sinks into my palm, my head pound-pounding.

'Are you okay?' Gloria doesn't want any trouble. We look like trouble, off kilter and what not.

'I'm hungry, that's all.'

'She wasn't asking you,' snarls Angel.

Don't get angry baby, get even. That's what I say. That's exactly why we're here.

'Fuck, Angel where was I?'

'You were about to silence Sal.'

Hell that was six weeks ago. Still can't believe what has happened. My entire life altered, scarcely recognize myself.

'What time is it?'

Angel checks her wristwatch but it stopped ages ago. 'Must be ten past two.'

The plan is to wait here for Fischer. Foolproof and simple: Fischer's to meet us here at three and then we'll drive over to Rob's. Rob, the target of my attentions, is going to get it tonight, get what's owed.

By this time tomorrow it will all be wrapped up. Finally I'll be able to put it all behind me, ready to start over fresh, for real this time. Ah what joy, what immense satisfaction shall be derived from finally seeing Rob come undone. I could get off just on the thought of it.

'Do you really think Fischer's going to show?'

'Angel. Five grand says he's definitely going to come.'

In the bag resting on my lap is ten grand. Five for Fischer and five for me. Taken off of Frank. Angel thinks I'm sick.

Maybe. Maybe I am.

'No Ed, I know you're sick.'

I stare her out, though she's right.

In the background Sal's favourite lyrics blare out: . . . *blame me, there's always me to blame . . . tra la la la . . .*

So for the last time . . .

She'd changed. Sal, that is. Physically. Her arse especially.

'You butt men . . .'

It had widened, softened and drooped.

'Angel,' and I tell her straight: 'None of your high moral crap, it happens all the time, in this day and age, a man's got to have some choices, a little bit of variety . . .'

A pretty piece of flesh

Angel yawns like she's heard it all before. Oh yeah, she's heard it all before.

'You cold Angel?'

I'm starting to feel cold, rub my hands together. Waiting on our meatballs, sat down the back, within minutes a host of draughts had emerged from the floor to hiss about us and unfurl a stench of dampness.

'Ed, what time is Fischer coming?'

'He said he'd be here around three.'

'You sure he's coming?'

'For chrissakes Angel, I'm positive.'

Angel's mouth twists taut, she's agitating me and knows it. She's been twittering on all day and there are times when I wish she'd shut her face, stop interrupting and her fat lip subside 'cause it makes her real ugly.

'Let's think about something else.'

'Tell me about the shampoo incident.'

'You want to hear it again?'

'Sure.' She nods.

Okay, so this happened, like six weeks ago. Sal was back at the flat and supposed to be going out later. She was trying on a dress bought a couple of years back. A dress I'd chosen for her. It had been purchased on one of those impulse shopping expeditions. I'd found it hanging half hidden at the back of the shop, mistakenly left on the bargain rail, when clearly it wasn't one, price tag in the hundreds. Sal had been ploughing through the rail, hoping to find that Extra Special Outfit, the one that's going make you feel like a million bucks. The one that hurls you from obscurity straight into a state of absolute gorgeousness. As if.

It was nice though, a slinky purple bias-cut dress that hugged Sal in all the right places and once in a while it's good to blow a bit of money. Pretend you are the master rather than the slave.

So, six weeks back, Sal stood in front of the full-length mirror, trying to push herself into this dress and bursting at the seams, the side stitching stretched tight.

'Sal, you can't go out in that. Look at you, you're looking kinda pudding, kinda slack.'

'Get lost, Ed.'

When you looked at Sal's face, up real close, you could see fine lines, you know, around the edges of her eyes and mouth. She was getting those little lines and her arse had gotten fat.

Angel says it was natural aging. I agree, sure, Sal had begun to look her age. Around the same time I'd spotted several grey hairs and torn them out of her head. I told her she should consider dying.

'You're getting grey hairs, Sal,' I said. 'Why don't you dye?'

When Sal was younger, she was beautiful. In her late teens, early twenties, before she met Rob.

It wasn't my fault she got lardy. It was part of the process. You know when she was like, twenty-two, maybe a little older, she had the longest, waviest hair. Softest hair, it was auburn and it used to fall all the way down her back, tickling the top of her round butt. Her sweet butt, she took it for granted. And she had this dolly face, like fucking beautiful.

She used to work the door at a hip club and guys, when they saw her, their jaws would drop and then they'd try to make smart-arse comments and their women, they'd just stare at her. In those days she'd walk around oblivious, totally unaware of the power of her aesthetic, of the power she could exert if she had wanted to. But that only added to the attraction.

In a nutshell, she was like the girl in the chocolate Flake commercial, perhaps a little bit ditsy.

I like to remember Sal in this way.

That night I was looking at Sal in the mirror. She was brushing her hair, now cut to a more practical shoulder length, clipping it back off her face in an attempt to cover up thirty years of experience, the last five permanently etched into her.

And then just as I'm in mid-flow, explaining the situation to Angel, she starts making noises, huffing and puffing,

'Why can't you guys accept the fact women age?'

'Why should we Angel?'

There, that's the truth of it. There's always someone else, prettier, fresher, not turned bitter by some wanker and they're all lined up and ready, waiting in the wings.

'So Ed, are you saying I'm fresher, is that what you're saying?'

'Sort of, yeah.'

Angel is mumbling under her breath, 'It's wrong, wrong, all wrong.'

She's pretty pure of intent is my Angel, and I respect that in her. Sal would have liked Angel, they may even have been best friends. Angel is a sweet cupcake with butterfly wings, or she would be if her blubber lip receded, her right cheek wasn't so swollen and the dirty bruises round her eyes weren't so obvious.

'Ed, do you think I'm pretty?'

Here we go and we all know what's coming next. Why is there always this need to seek approval?

'Angel,' I sigh, 'you're smart, smart enough not to let what happened to Sal, happen to you.'

'Ed, you're avoiding the question,' and she repeats it. 'Am I pretty? Am I really pretty, the prettiest, the most beautiful girl in the world, the one from Ipanema, heart and ballbreaker, the one and only, am I, am I?

'Angel,' and I feel obliged to be honest, 'you look kinda freakish at the moment.'

Bubba, bubba and this sets her off, a fat teardrop squeezes out of her lid and down her face. So much for honesty and I pass her a crappy serviette out of the dispenser. The sort that are about as absorbent as cling film. She slides me a look of both grief and disgust. I try to change the subject and start on again about the shampoo incident.

Sal stood in front of the mirror, smudging foundation over her face, matching skin tones and she was meant to be going out later. In that dress. Her fleshed squeezed in tight, so you could see the zip seam stretched out.

'How do I look?' Sal asked, pulling at the material trying to expand it.

'Fat.'

'Thanks Ed.'

'Well, there's no point lying to yourself.'

Angel interrupts, reckons I was jealous of Rob. Jealous isn't the right word. I loathe the guy. Absolutely and totally.

'And stop interrupting me Angel, or we aren't going to get anywhere fast.'

'I never said a thing.'

'Don't answer me back. Look, I'd totally had enough of Sal and that's why I had to get rid of her.'

'Just stick to the facts,' says Angel.

It was a Tuesday evening and Sal arrived home in a mood. The first day of the new year and she'd spent it trawling Oxford Street in search of bargains and ending up buying nothing. Tossing her bag by the door, she threw her jacket on the bed and then plonked down in front of the 21-inch telly to watch *Emmerdale*. She was munching on a Mars bar, a solid bar of saturated fat.

This is how Sal eats – Correction, this was how Sal ate her Mars bar:

She'd pull back the wrapper revealing about an inch of the bar, then nibble the layer of chocolate till the insides were exposed. Next she'd lick the caramel off the whisked crap, which she'd then suck on. It was an art she practised most evenings, ensuring the bar would last the whole length of the soap episode. Then she'd light a fag.

'Think of all the calories Sal, I mean you aren't exactly doing yourself any favours here.' Time and again I'd warned her.

'Ed, leave me alone.' We were having relationship problems.

The phone rang, interrupting my rant. Sal answered.

'Hello?'

'Hi Sal, how's it going?' My ear pressed next to hers. It was Rob.

'Hey Rob.'

Standing behind her I whispered, 'Put the phone down, Sal.'

'Fuck off, Ed.'

'Put the phone down, Sal.'

'Fuck you, Ed.'

A three-way conversation, her other ear practically sucking up Rob's vocal tones.

'You busy tonight?' Rob asked.

'No, why?'

'Fancy a visit?'

'Yeah, okay.'

The bitch. This is the kinda shit I had to put up with. And it was, may I add, only the tip of the iceberg.

'See you round nine.'

'Great,' and Sal put down the receiver, her cheeks flushed crimson.

So she had pulled out the dress, the one I chose for her that time we'd gone shopping, the dress she couldn't fit in anymore and then went to take a shower.

Standing in the bathroom, in her pants and bra that had been washed to grey, she checked her pits for hair growth and then her legs, testing a silk scarf to see would it fall down unhindered. I followed her in there and told her straight.

'You can't keep doing this to me. It's over, Sal. Look at you. Look at yourself. At what you've become.'

'Ed, I'm not going through this anymore.'

I could make her cry. It was easy, like a war of attrition, undermining her till she'd stop whatever she was doing and take a look at herself. I mean, there was a time when she could have had anyone she wanted.

'Remember all those plans we used to have, the dreams we shared?'

'No,' she snapped.

'Liar.'

*

Sal and I went way back, almost to the beginning. Fuck, I remember when she first grew tits, swollen little nipples, soft tufts of hair sprouting under her arms and then below. The very beginning of her adolescent self-conscious period. We grew up together, same street, same school, same social milieu and drifted in and out of each other's lives. Warming our backs on the school radiators, dreaming away our future. Hey, we were going to experience so many different things, go on these crazy journeys, the only thing ever stopping us was Sal.

The joy was gone, the blush of youth had left behind a pallor and she kept on screwing with my head. I couldn't bear it any longer.

Naked, she was all soap sudded. I watched as she fumbled, eyes wet, reaching out for a shampoo. Hint of a tint, coloured to cover those stray grey hairs. I used to pluck them out for her. I had bought Sal a bottle of shampoo, auburn tinted 'cause her hair was all tired and lacklustre, cut to her shoulders, practical, not like when it lapped all the way down her back, in soft crescent waves.

'I can't continue like this Sal.' I swear I did my best to put it to her straight.

Tra la la you don't want me, need me, care . . . makes me love you more and more.

She sang flat and out of tune.

'He doesn't love you Sal.'

Tra la la . . . Doing her best to ignore me.

'Not like I do.'

See, Sal knew in her heart of hearts it was over.

'I've had such a shit day Ed,' she moaned.

'I think I'm going to have to kill you Sal.'

And she started to snivel.

Okay, I didn't exactly say that. Those weren't my exact words.

She was standing in the shower with a gob of shampoo in her hand and she began to lather it into her hair, rubbing foamed fingers through her scalp.

This was when I took the decision. I suspect it had been a long time gestating, right at the back of my mind, latent, unlabelled – and we're talking years here. Could never quite articulate it, then I guess it must have ripened and suddenly, I knew I had to put a stop to what was going on.

Rinsing out the shampoo, she stood beneath the shower, letting the water pelt down on her, as if it could really clean up the mess we found ourselves in. Sal was sullied and no matter how hard she rubbed at the dirt it had gotten inside, deep down in the pores, where the filth was self-perpetuating. I was going to have to do it.

'Ed, I'm not really getting this,' says Angel.

I'm trying to be as clear as possible, but the last six weeks has blurred everything, so that it's all steamed up in my head.

'Okay Angel, I'll talk a little slower.'

Relaxing back on the pew in Gloria's, doing my best to explain the situation to Angel.

I was looking at Sal in the shower, the idea coming to fruition. How can I put it? It was as if all the time the solution had been staring me straight in the face. I handed Sal a towel as she stepped out of the shower. I was going to have to get rid of her.

'But why?' asks Angel.

'Because my sweet, as the commercial goes, as the girl

looks to the camera and flicks back her super shiny hair, she was worth it.'

Ten things I hated about Sal.

1. Her breath. Her stomach was all mucked up, too much acid or alkaline. It would hang there on the out breath. She'd suck on mints or chew gum but there was always a trace of stagnation.

2. Her timekeeping. She always managed to be late. This may have been endearing in the early years, when she could pass it off, but these days it was just damn tiresome.

3. The lying. The tight reins of self-deception. Standing in the dress, thinking she looked nice, when the reality was stretching the truth a long way.

4. Her addiction to trash. Music, books, third-rate TV sitcoms, dulling her into a stupor.

5. Her unquestioning acceptance of everything and loss of her dreams. Here was someone who'd spent hours in her youth in front of the mirror flirting with herself, mouthing the words, 'I am a star, I AM A STAR'. Christ she could have shone, she had this smile, so sexy so . . . and a glow in her eyes. Shit – you'd surrender to this woman, you'd bring your mother to meet her. Then she sort of gave up, succumbed to mediocrity, to dumbing down, erosion of self-expectation, leading to –

6. Her unerring belief in the system. She bought all the lies, she got fat on them, she got fucked on them. Cheesy music, microwave meals, relationship novels about single women meeting Mr Right, then Mr Wrong then finally Mr Right and her growing reliance on self-fucking-help manuals.

7. Her obvious spiritual, emotional and physical decay.

That's only seven.

8. Rob.

9. Rob.

10. Rob.

There, that's ten.

She was still screwing Rob.

There, now you know. She was fucking Rob.

Not to mention Frank.

As a man, I ask you honestly, would you just stand there and take that kind of shit?

Really, could you? Now, do you get the picture?

'So it wasn't just that she was losing her looks?' Angel stops me with another question.

I'd thought about it. 'She'd already lost her looks. That was a mere manifestation of the problem.'

'I'm glad you said that,' snorts Angel, ' 'cause I was thinking, that's a really shallow reason to kill someone. It would make you appear somewhat psychotic.'

Sometimes I think I'm obsessed by the superficial.

'Maybe it's the visual age we live in.'

'Oh here we go, blah, blah, vent, vent.' Angel's taking the piss. It doesn't bother me in the slightest, she knows she has to listen to me.

'Angel hear me out. Say for instance, you open the paper and read how an eighteen-year-old was murdered . . .'

I raise my palm to curtail another Angel attempted interruption.

'If the victim is this sweet looking thing, pretty, innocent, you feel bad. What a waste, how sad you think. If, on the other hand, the victim had pig features you skip the article and read about some heroic feat of a family pet.'

Angel throws her eyes up to heaven. 'Ed I hate when you spout shit like that.'

'But Angel it's true.'

She looks away, conscious once more of her own battered face. She looks away and then looks down. Taking a sugar packet from out of the stainless steel tumbler, she tears it open and dabbing her little finger in the pack, then presses some sweetness on to her lips. Angel's gone all sulky on me.

And I'm the first to admit that at times I can be such an asshole.

The day I did Sal in was a Wednesday and we were in the flat in Kentish Town. A council flat, sub-let off a Scottish lass, who five years previously had gone back to Glasgow with her kid. It was a nice size for one, bit of a crush for two and we'd get on top of one another. We didn't hear from the Scot much, once a year, she rarely came visiting. Then, out of the blue, she had called by with her kid, now seven, and her new boyfriend, Roger.

'Just down in London for the weekend, on a pre-Chrissy shopping trip, thought we'd pop by.' So they said, or words to that effect. So we all have tea and biscuits, it was very civilized.

'I like what you've done to the flat Sal. It looks really nice,' enthused Coleen.

Roger was scanning the place like a one-man drugs squad, opening every cupboard, every drawer.

Then a couple of weeks later we received a call, notifying us of our immediate eviction. Two days given to quit said premises. 'Gosh, but we really like what you've done to the flat Sal.'

Nothing lasts forever.

Coleen, shrewd as you like, passing the buck, her fella obviously pressurizing her and she's full of Roger this, Roger that, Roger's spawn in her pale pig-bloat of a belly.

'We've decided to give London another go. You understand don't you?' The call came on that Wednesday morning, Sal dabbing at the edges of her eyes, already in a bit of a state. The answerphone kicked in and she couldn't believe what she was hearing, jumped up and ran to it.

She grabbed the handset: 'Coleen?'

'Oh . . . you're in, I thought you'd be at work.' Apparently, Coleen was hoping she would get away with leaving us a message. 'You're not sick are you?' she asked.

'No, what's this about you coming down?'

'Yeah, look Sal, sorry about the short notice an'all, but we're moving back to London this coming weekend. We'll need the flat.'

The import of what Coleen was saying began to strike home. Sal pulled up her forehead, exposing her ridges. She snatched a cigarette from her pack and tried to light it.

'Are you saying I've got to move?'

'I'm sorry Sal . . .'

Okay, first off, you got to understand that when Coleen had left the flat, it was a tip, a dump, a damp shithole.

Five years back they had met by chance. Sal, on her way home from work was heading to her water aerobics class at the Kentish Town pool when, on the Castlehaven Road, she fatefully runs into Coleen with her kid, then aged two, blocking up the pavement. Coleen's shopping bags had burst open, groceries scattered at her feet. The kid was screaming, pulling away from his mum 'cause she had her hands clasped round his throat and was throttling him. She'd lost it. Coleen screeching at full lung capacity, *Shut up, shut the fuck up, shut up*. Sal to her rescue, Sal being an inherently decent person. 'It's okay,' and Sal peels back Coleen's fingers from around the kid's neck and wraps Coleen in her own arms in an effort to quell her rage.

Sal took Coleen home, listened to her tale of woe; pregnant at sixteen, boyfriend fled, leaving her dependent on the state, staunch Catholic parents in Glasgow, unaware of her plight and she had slowly been cracking up. Sal empathized, sympathized, and out of the goodness of her heart for the next month looked after Coleen and the kid. They bonded, became good friends and Sal moved in. Connection with Coleen's parents was re-established and they rushed down to London to see the grandchild they knew nothing about. A short while after, Coleen went back to Glasgow for a week, which turned into a month, which then turned into five years. Sal remained in the flat, aware one day she would have to give it back, but there was no rush and the rent was reasonable and always paid on time.

Then came the knock on the door. Hello, hello, and Sal was genuinely pleased to see Coleen, big hug, big kiss, my, my, would you look at how much Kevin has grown, and who's this great thuggish hulk standing at your side . . . Roger . . . how nice to meet you.

'Gosh and would you look at *my* flat. It's lovely, you've done wonders to it Sal.'

True, Sal had gotten comfortable, made the place a home, painted it, decorated it, coated the walls in her hard earned cash. She'd installed a whole new kitchen, brand new bathroom, spanking new power shower. Fixed the place up so it looked real pretty, Ikea assembled, of the moment, straight out of a magazine, colour by numbers.

Put it together and what have you got?

DIY.

Now sound it phonetically. It had become a situation in which I had to take control.

So Coleen called, hoping she wouldn't find Sal in and thus casually serve us an eviction notice. *What a spa?*

'I understand it's short notice but Roger says . . . look we need the flat back Sal.'

'Sorry, when did you say you're coming?'

'This weekend.'

'What!'

'Roger has a job down in London, starting next week.'

'I would have thought you could've given me more time.'

Coleen's guilt and embarrassment were making her defensive. Her tone edged with impatient anger. 'Look, there's nothing I can do about it. Roger wants to come down this weekend.'

In the background I fumed. Put Coleen onto me. I was riled, they're fucking us over royally Sal.

'Put her on to me.' I was steaming at the nostrils.

Meanwhile, Sal had burst out crying and was apologizing to Coleen.

'It's just a bit of a shock. It's going to be really hard to find somewhere else in a couple of days.'

'Something will come up, it always does.' And the conversation ended there.

I slapped my forehead, wanting to slap some sense into Sal

before she shrivelled up into a weepy ball of woe and what's going to become of me. Accepting the inevitable, I was seething with her, couldn't she see Coleen was way out of order.

'But it's her flat,' Sal whimpered, already defeated.

'What about human decency? Don't you get it? They came by the flat, saw what you'd done to it and the next minute they're on their way down. Can't you see Sal? What's happening here is we are being fucked over.'

We had a bust up. I was gaining the upper hand. At last, I got to have a say and I may as well tell you now, it had been a long time coming.

Sal would never listen to me. She had the art of ignoring my voice down to a tee. Any manner of things used as a distraction, especially music, dumb pop tunes played real loud to drown out the background interference of my voice.

That was one of the major problems of our relationship. Communication. It's all down to communication.

I was screaming at her, 'When woman, when are you going to listen to me?' Shoving her up against the wall, snatching the dead phone from out of her hand.

I called Coleen and told her straight out I'd ring the council, told her she'd lose her flat unless she gave us a month's notice.

'You can't treat people like this.'

'It's my flat. I can do what I want.'

'Is it? Is it really your flat, well let's see what the council think after five years of sub-letting it.'

'I want my flat back.'

'Coleen, I don't care, the least you could do is give us a month's notice.'

'It's my flat . . .'

She was screaming Armageddon. *Whah, whah, fucking whah.*

'A month's notice. Take it or leave it.'

'I'm going to see what Roger has to say about this.'

'Yeah and you tell Roger to call me.'

Half an hour later Roger called, threat, threat, he's gonna break my legs, he's going smash me up, he's going to frighten me into submission.

'Roger I'm calling the council.'

'You do and you're dead.'

Yeah, yeah, pal you're talking to Ed here.

Coleen called back. 'Sal you bitch, you conniving bitch. Roger's right, you wheedled your way into my flat when I was at my most vulnerable. Taking it over, well fuck you, I want you out by tomorrow and Roger is on his way down to London now.'

This for me was the final straw. There was no way I was going to carry Sal any longer.

This happened on Wednesday. The day I ended up killing her. The night before, Sal had squeezed herself into a purple dress, a size too small and waited for Rob. She stood by the mirror trying to hide the black rings under her eyes and fade out the fine lines. I'd begged her not to see him.

'It's nothing.'

'He's your ex for God's sake.'

'Don't you trust me?'

'Frankly . . .'

'Oi darlin,' Gloria barks.

Outside the rain continues to fall. A howling wind has set up, blustering against the sides of the shed.

'Food's ready.'

I shuffle over to the counter to collect our meatballs. Angel admitted to being a vegetarian before we met. Figures. Facing me is a humble plate of tomato slop, meat mush. Splish splash. Sticky boil in the bag rice with the excess starch water framing the edge of the dish. I catch sight of the empty can, brand 'X' meatballs, in tomato glup with a staggering 33% extra free. Gloria's plates are paper weight and have a translucent quality, cheap and nasty.

I order a Coke.

Gloria hands me a Pepsi. I rise to the challenge.

'This isn't Coke.'

'We only have Pepsi.' Gloria's response dispatched as a warning.

'I asked for a Coke.'

'What do you want me to do about it?'

'Well what else do you have?'

'Lilt, Fanta, water.'

I can tell my presence is beginning to annoy Gloria.

Gloria wears rings on every finger. I have an inkling she's a woman with tattoos up her arm. Though none are visible, I suspect they lie hidden beneath her Christmas-patterned, woollen jumper. A large cross dangles from her neck and her multi-pierced ears are studded in different coloured glass; gold, orange, blue, green, black. I reckon on her being around fifty, though she may be younger. Crouched over the fridge freezer, I can hear her mumbling under her breath. 'You can't tell the difference.'

Her eyes meet mine. 'Pepsi, that's it, take it or leave it.'

I feel like drinking Coke.

Three photos are tacked to the wall next to a free calendar –

Syntax Technologies – January's picture showed an orbiting space satellite in a night sky. The photos reveal glimpses of Gloria's existence; the first being Gloria stood beside the TV presenter Cilla Black, the second Gloria sitting on the knee of the big bloke from Meatloaf and the third was of a proud cabbie stood next to his car, who I presume is her husband.

'Are you okay?' she enquires.

I had leant my full weight on the counter and unsecured, it shifted a bit.

'Tired,' I yawn. 'It's a dreadful night out there.'

Stating the obvious, hoping to appease her inquisitive stare. She isn't convinced by me. I can tell Gloria wants us out of her catering shed.

'When are you expecting Boris?'

Boris!

Fischer never told me his name was Boris. Guess I never asked, he'd introduced himself as Fischer and that was enough. He didn't look like a Boris. His hands weren't hairy and his beardline didn't rise from his chest to meet his jaw. Boris! Jesus, what kind of cruel mother did he have, one with a sick sense of humour, a crush on Karloff.

'He won't be too long, said he'd be here around three.'

Gloria glances up at the clock, a plastic blue fish, stuck to the side wall between two windows. It's only twenty past two. We've at least, presuming Fischer comes on time, three quarters of an hour together, though a night like this is bound to be busy. He'll be prone to delays what with every-one wanting shelter from the elements. Fischer's one of those types, old fashioned I guess, who has a heart, you know like a fairly decent, honest person. Totally freaked me when I first met him. Anyhow it will screw things up if he's late.

Fish Clock

A couple of days ago I revealed my plan and offered Fischer five thousand for half an hour's work. Not bad eh?

He'd grunted, unenthralled, then tried on some old style bartering. 'Six,' he demanded.

'Forget it.'

I wasn't in the mood to bargain. He was in or he was out, fifty-fifty, take it or leave it. After all I was the one who had secured the ten grand cash. An undertaking not easily achieved, having had to be unscrupulous in disengaging it from the hands of Frank, Sal's ex-boss.

Disgusted, I had turned my back on Fischer, stormed down the piss-stinking hallway out of his flat knowing he'd follow.

I'd been staying at his place for the previous few days, chucking vodka back, then forth, and hearing the whole of Fischer's life story in detail, especially the plummeting bit, from esteemed Soviet doctor to London mini-cab driver, didn't even own his car, in debt, a sick mother and family to keep back in Moscow. There was no way he'd turn my offer down. There was no need to bargain.

So Fischer came running after me, down the stairwell, huffing and puffing. I marched stridently onward.

'Okay, okay. I'll take it,' he gasped.

I swung round, he was perspiring, his high forehead gleaming and a cigarette hanging off his lower lip.

'Okay, five thousand, it's a deal.' He was in.

I spat into my hand, presented my moistened palm and we shook. A deal was struck.

'You and I,' mused Fischer, 'We are a lot alike,' and parting his lips, he exposed his remaining wealth. Then to re-emphasize the point his clenched fist thumped against his chest. 'Spirit, soul.' Each word pronounced with a singular reverence.

He flung his arm over my shoulder and we went back up to his flat.

I'm almost certain Gloria thinks I'm a sad case, a probable runaway who should be in a homeless hostel. In the circumstances not a bad guess. A look of disgust flares across her face and I imagine she thinks she's worked it out; Boris paying to do it with me, and/or Angel – hey, there's a thought. She hadn't suspected he was one of them, of that ilk. Imagine if she knew there was ten grand sitting on her stool. She wouldn't believe me if I told her; if she's nice to me I'll leave her a generous tip.

There I go running to conclusions, not such a good thing; before you know it, you'll get beyond yourself. I should know, having done just that.

Sal was my conclusion.

Yes, in retrospect I must confess that it's opened up a whole new landscape in which to play. More has happened to me in the last six weeks than in the same number of years. It's frightening even to think in those terms, that you can drift for so long without actually taking control. Sal had become one of those people who would never take responsibility, *I was only doing my duty, baa, baa.* Bullshit.

'Do you want the Pepsi or not?' Gloria hisses, impatient to sit down again and take the weight off her feet. 'Well?'

I grab the can, fix it under my chin, get the food and return to my Angel.

With Sal dead nothing seemed to matter anymore. Having given myself free scope to do whatever I wanted I went a little loco, but at last, an end is in sight. A final showdown beckons, myself versus Rob, nothing as romantic as swords at dawn, he hasn't got a clue what I've planned.

Tomorrow, I'll be in Paris, I have the tickets on me. From there we'll head down to Barcelona. I'll see, the future's vague, one step at a time.

And I truly believe I'm doing it for Sal. For me and I guess, at a push, for Angel too.

Poor Rob, he's in for a surprise and not a particularly nice one at that, but fitting all the same. There's nothing to lose, I'm so far in I can't go much further. And I know Sal would have wanted it like this. To settle her debts and clean slate her existence.

What you have to understand is, that even when I really hated Sal, when I detested her very being, I still loved her. If anything I regard what I did as her salvation.

Now, I dunno, maybe I feel a sense of sorrow. A smidgen of compassion. I blame it on Angel. Yeah, it was a pity things got so out of hand.

Angel has a headache. I pass her a paracetamol or three. Her nose begins to run and she takes a deep sniff.

'Don't say you've caught a cold, my Angel.'

Angel reminds me that I skipped the bit about Rob, what happened on that Tuesday night. The too tight dress night.

'I'll get to it, Angel.' Jesus give me a break. 'I'm trying to digest dogfood here.'

My empty stomach aching. The pitfalls of being a renegade.

Tuesday night, six weeks back and Sal had received a call from Rob, her ex.

I knew all there was to know about Rob 'cause I got to wipe up the leftovers, as usual. I'd watched from the sidelines at a safe distance. I was the steady friend, the bad-patch buddy, the cried-on shoulder, hoping for more. They were together three years and she'd hoped for a fairytale ending, to one day marry him, have his kiddies and settle down. They met when she was twenty-five and her hair hung halfway down her back. She had given up doing the door at the club Zipload, in preference for a proper job and began to work for a TV production company.

Sal was a smart girl, one of those people who, if they put their mind to it, could do anything they wanted. Sal's only trouble being that she was unsure, what, exactly, that was. So she began working as a research assistant for a third-rate TV company, applied herself admirably and within a year and a half was a production assistant at Tack TV. The company specialized in trendy wank, fly on the wall docusoaps revealing as much as possible to titillate the socially unconscious. Stuff like, 'Swinging sixties – pensioners and sex', 'Your mother's a whore – mine really is', 'Thank heavens for little girls – an in-depth look at the continued sacrifice of virgins'.

Rob, a freelance producer, had been called in to work on the project 'Dada wears nappies'. He was twenty-seven, arrogant, determined and had the face of a God. Bar his age, he still is all those things. His appeal was instant; every woman in the company, even the token dyke, fawned over the guy. His desk was always cluttered with freshly made coffee, laughter, gossip and perched rears in tight skirts, hiked up, revealing a tad too much leg. He had ivy looks that latched on and grew, would lock eyes with you when talking, one on one, showing a sensitivity not usually associated with the male of the species. He could wrap you round his finger and tie you in a bow, male or female. If I didn't despise him, I would want to fuck him too. That kind of guy.

Sal ignored him. Already smitten, she was pretending to dislike him in that inverse way of trying to gain some attention.

He asked her one day, 'Sal, have I done something to offend you?'

'No, no why would you think that?'

He mentioned the fact he was starting on another project the following week. 'I'm leaving on Friday, we're going for some drinks.'

Keep them waiting, never be an eager beaver lady, on Guides' honour play it cool.

Thinking about it for a moment she replied, 'Sorry, I can't make it. Got a date.'

'Maybe another time,' and he left it at that.

This occurred during the period when Sal was at the peak of her desirability. She had at her disposal numerous possibilities, a small legion of admirers gagging to take her out and win her over. At the time a young music video director was the recipient of her casual affections. A stop-gap sort of guy, the type you date when there's no one else and who has access to a load of great parties. She met Rob again on one such occasion and that's how it started for real.

Sal fell in love big time.

I always had to take second place to Rob. He had cut into Sal deep, whereas I merely licked the wounds. If Sal hadn't treated me so bad things could have been different.

To be honest I didn't get it. After everything that had gone on between the two of them, I failed to understand why she hadn't completely severed the ties. It disgusted me the way he'd drop by from time to time. Dip in, so to speak.

Rob called by on the Tuesday evening.

Over her shoulder I sneered.

'It's finished Sal.'

'Whatever, Ed.'

'It's over Sal. I'm through with you. You can't do this to me any longer.' I spelt it out to her.

She claimed to be dyslexic.

Rob rang the buzzer, Sal buzzed him in and I buzzed off.

I knew what would happen, their little routine . . .

'Hey babe,' and Rob would bend forward to kiss her on those lips of hers, my lips, my Sal. Rob addressed all females in terms of mock endearment, love, sugar, sweetie, whatever.

Rob would appraise her. 'Like your dress, the colour suits you.'

Couldn't the dick see it was two sizes too small?

'Come here,' and she'd go to him. He could have just as easily whistled or clicked his fingers. A person can only take so much abuse.

'How's things?' Throwing off his jacket, collapsing down on her snug two-seater.

'Work's a drag, Frank's still being a complete slime.'

Frank was Sal's boss of four years, a lecherous type, with a penchant for rubbing up behind her, or any cute-assed assistant, preferably female, though on one occasion he'd made an error, a 'do you remember the time Frank . . .' story that would follow him to his retirement and beyond.

'Why don't you look for another job?' Rob suggested this on every visit but Sal was comfortable where she was, any ambition sapped by the relative ease of a good salary, flashy work environment, occasional perks and perpetual laziness.

And every time Sal would answer, 'Suppose you're right.'

'So Rob, what do you want to do tonight?' Sal all coy, in her too-tight dress, like a born again virgin.

That look, that smirk on his face, Sal standing opposite with a hand on her hip.

'Mmm, don't mind.' The empty space to his side.

Sal sliding down next to him, 'You want a drink?'

'Nah,' his hand sliding up under her dress, towards her crotch, leaning in and starting to kiss her.

The bastard. Should've gone for him then. Should have put a stop to the whole damn situation.

Then and there and the next thing you know, she's doing it with him, they'd be at it. My stomach churning. Rob on top on her. All over her. It makes me sick just thinking about it. She was so damn eager to please.

I can't do it, trawl through the details like a pornographer, I'd only be beating myself up and the stupid dress was hanging off the sofa, half on the Ikea modern patterned rug. Hump, hump, enough.

Then Rob's mobile ting-a-ling, a-lings, interrupting them mid coitus and this was what happened.

He still had his socks on.

Get this, Sal has the foresight to turn down the music, Zucchero's 'Feels Like a Woman', suspecting in advance it would be his girlfriend.

Rob grabs his jacket, his hand reaching into the inside pocket and out pops a microscopic phone, the tiniest on the market and he snaps open the technology, motioning Sal to silence.

'Hey,' he says. 'Hey babe, what's up?'

Yabba, yabba and he's playing with Sal's tits talking to his girlfriend on his mobile.

'Sure I'll be home in a while,' he says.

Sal's stroking his dick, like this is cool.

'Hey angel, almost forgot, Milo's offered us his villa in the Bahamas, for the honey . . . let's talk about it later. Okay . . . yeah I'm held up in traffic . . . aha . . . on my way. At the most an hour.'

Phone flicked shut and then he's back to doing what he does best. Screwing with people.

The idea repulses me, even thinking about it gives me the heebie jeebies.

He jumped off her, pulled up his jeans. 'I'm going to have to go,' nonchalantly stated, bare chested and sexy with it. Strutting around her small living room all dick satiated.

Sal didn't bother with the dress, instead she sloped off to the bathroom and reappeared in her towelling robe, tying the belt.

'I thought we were going out.'

'Sorry babe, another time.' He was rooting in Sal's fridge for a drink or something.

'Oh,' said Sal. 'Really I thought you said we were going out.'

'Sal, I get enough grief at home,' and Rob put a stop to the conversation. 'She's on one at the moment. How come my girlfriends are always so insecure?'

''Cause you encourage it,' answered Sal.

'But you should see the ring I got her.'

Sal hadn't expected this response. 'What's that?'

'Didn't I tell you? we're getting married. Proposed on Christmas Eve.' Rob was buttoning up his flies.

'Sweetie,' and he looked up at Sal. 'Don't worry, you're on the invite list.'

The meatballs have stuck in my throat, I cough up some grains of rice. When Sal broke up from Rob, all I got was, Rob, Rob, why? why? It was off-putting to say the least, yet all the while she remained blind to the fact that it was me who really loved her. It was me who'd look after her.

He'd fuck my girl and I had to clean up the mess.

Sometimes I'd wonder why he kept her on. Because she was a great lay? Yeah she was damn sexy, but it was more a power trip for Rob, a chance to inflate his dick-ego.

I was enraged; tell me, honestly – could you have held back?

Every time Sal ended up with Rob, I'd tell her it was over. Again and again but she never listened. Each infidelity puncturing me, so that my legs buckled under and motionless, I was stuck in this situation. I could never leave, such was my dependence on Sal. I remember confiding all this to a phone tarot card operator who in the end told me to 'get a life'. I did just that.

Though in retrospect, my conduct may appear premeditated, it wasn't. I'd merely come to understand what was bubbling beneath the skin. When you love someone and they start messing you round, and you've been together years, it's easy to find excuses and forgiveness for such actions. You rationalize, redefining infidelity, so that you don't differentiate between a thought and an action, 'cause then it's easier to bear.

How many times a day for example, do you drool, ache, admire another, other than your partner? Minor visual and cerebral flirtations, are they not imaginary infidelities? And the leap to reality is barely any distance. Sal would cry, 'I swear, I'll never do it again, I swear this time was the last.' And I loved her so much I believed it. I desperately wanted to. She was everything to me. Casting yourself upon the one person you have invested your whole self in, your hopes, desires, dreams and I clung to the thought of one day when my sense of apparent acceptance and subordination would be rewarded.

Look, I was cracking up, cards stacked one on top of each other, ready to topple. Sure anyone with any kind of cop could have predicted what was going to happen.

Rob helped himself to the last fag from Sal's open packet, her pre-bedtime ritual one, smoked standing up beside the kitchen sink, after she'd brushed her teeth.

Sucking in the smoke, looking like some James Dean make-over, Rob said, 'Sal, you look sad.'

'I thought we were going out.'

'Not that again. I came over didn't I?'

'Guess so.'

'Shit you're not going to start crying, are you?'

She tried to dam the tears, turning her face away from him.

'So,' she ventured doing her utmost to sound all casual, 'when's the big day?'

'Around six weeks,' he replied nonchalantly, stubbing out the cigarette in a Quaglino's ashtray, purchased, not nicked, a souvenir of happier times with Rob.

'Yep, I surrender, I'm finally going to get hitched. Look I got to go babe, otherwise she'll get suspicious. Catch you later.'

He tousled her hair before closing the door and letting himself out.

In the meantime, I'd scooted down to Patel's newsagents, to buy some cigarettes, splashed out on a packet of twenty. Patel proudly announced his daughter had just graduated with a first in Law from Middlesex university. Like at that moment I gave a shit.

How could Sal do it?

Slow-paced it back to the flats, looking out for Rob's car but already it had gone. With the keys gripped in my hand, I'd imagined scratching WANKER across the shiny silver BMW bonnet.

My sight levitated two flights up, to the flat, confirming my suspicions; the light was on and Sal was in. I knew they wouldn't have gone out, they never did. I could almost make out Sal by the kitchen window.

On my return Sal didn't say much, didn't have to. She stood by the kitchen sink and smoked fifteen fags, one after another until she eventually ran to the toilet to puke.

The next day, the Wednesday, Sal stayed home. You should have seen the state she was in.

*

Angel sniffs, 'So she was upset about Rob getting married?'

'Haven't you listened to a word I've said Angel?'

Sal was devastated, she'd always thought they would get back together.

'So what did you do?'

Let's skip ahead . . .

I got an axe. Damn thing was heavy in my hands. I got an axe and wielded it high above my head.

The first thing I did after wiping out Sal. My girl Sal. In case of emergency break glass. I broke the glass and I got the key and snatched the axe from the maintenance cupboard down the hallway, then I ran back to the flat.

Five years of accumulated comfort and we had been given zero notice. That very morning Coleen had called to evict us. I wasn't having that. I went into the kitchen, lovely wooden kitchen, fake country rustic, ten feet square. Petite and cutesy, with careful planning enough room for a sweet table. Walls painted a primrose morning, a clean plate draining on the Habitat wooden draining board, white painted wooden chairs with pretty little cushions tied on. Fridge face obscured by photos of great times out with mates. Moments to remember, I'm up there, smiling and laughing. Floorboards exposed, sanded and varnished a blue hue to match the kitchen blind.

Wood, wood, wood and there I was chop, chop, chopping.

Five years in the making and I should know, having had a hand in it.

Wonderful shelving but what goes up, must come down. MDF is easy peasy pudding and pie. Get this, the upstairs neighbour started banging on the wall, to keep the noise down, no hammering after eleven.

The weird dopehead neighbour, spliffed out of it and it got me thinking I could do with some . . .

I laid down the axe. I was shaking, sweated up and climbed one flight of stairs, to knock on his door. I could hear voices from inside, the shuffling of feet, someone creeping up to the spyhole, checking out who it was.

I eased the corners of my mouth out wide, in a friendly manner, and the door opened slightly, a chink from which the smell of sweet grass emerged to then swim up my moist nostrils.

'Hi, I'm your neighbour from downstairs.'

'Yeah?'

'Sorry about the noise and all.'

'I'm trying to relax up here.'

'I was thinking . . .' Bear in mind I'd just gotten rid of Sal, I'd just smashed up her dream kitchen.

'What?' He peered through the door, his eyelids half closed over, 'You're letting in a draught.'

'Can I come in?'

'What's your name?'

'Ed.'

He popped his head out from behind the door, swinging it one way then the other, checking the length of the corridor. It was plain, even in my state, that he was odd in a mental health sort of way.

He pushed the door open a little more; I attempted wedging my way through, but got stuck in the middle. He whispered in my ear.

'Gotcha.'

'Ha, bloody ha, just open the fucking door.'

'You the one who lives downstairs?' he asked. 'You look different.'

'Yeah, well what can I say?'

'My name's Neville.'

Neville stood in jockey shorts and an old Stussy t-shirt. He was tall and gangly, with scabs on his legs. He rubbed his hand over his crotch and walked ahead of me into the sitting room. His flat was sparsely furnished. He told me to keep the noise down 'cause his mother was sleeping. First I'd heard of any mother, I'd always assumed he lived on his own. There was a large DVD TV set and mega sound system, three hardbacked chairs and a brown corduroy beanbag. A low, smoked-glass-topped coffee-table was pushed up against the wall with a stuffed plump Safeway's plastic bag resting on top. A quick glance inside confirmed the contents.

'You want a smoke?'

'Sure.'

'Smoke till you choke,' and he chuckled at what I guessed was an attempt at humour. The guy's brains were fried, though he seemed harmless enough. His eyes kept darting in their sockets and he sat astride one of the hardbacked chairs and switched on the TV.

'Who wants to be a millionaire?' He rocked back in the chair, 'I do, I do,' answering himself and we sat watching the quiz show while I indulged in some ganja. Neville attempted every quiz question, failing to get a single one right and this amused me no end. With each wrong reply, he'd slap his forehead and go 'Duh!', Homer Simpson style.

I began laughing, was soon doubled over by the pain in my belly, my eyes were streaming and then I began to cough.

'Smoke till you choke.'

Duh, hahahahahahahahaha.

*

'Sorry Ed, you've lost me again,' Angel butts in.

'We're on the night I killed Sal, after smashing up her dream kitchen.'

I'd despair but there'd be no point. I can tell Angel's shattered. She's been yawning these last five minutes, the warmth of the food urging her to relax a little. It hurts to stretch her jaw and her head sinks into her small hands, elbows propped up on either side.

Stroking her hair, I murmur, 'Hey Angel, don't you remember? Wednesday, the day Coleen called and evicted us from the flat. Sal had flipped. You should have seen the state she was in.'

Sometimes I think if I hadn't done it, destroyed her, Sal would have done it to herself.

Tuesday night Rob had called round and fucked Sal. She hardly slept after Rob left, having informed her of his impending nuptials. She tossed and turned in bed. 'Ed, don't you have anything to say?' she was taunting me. 'Come on Ed, surely you of all people have something to say about this.'

'It's over Sal. I've told you a million times before.' She wanted me to sympathize, make her feel better.

I turned away, me ignoring *her* this time.

'Come on Ed, rub it in.'

'Go to sleep Sal.'

'I'm waiting Ed, it's not like you.'

I lay there, all the while aware Rob was still inside her, his stuff, warm and alive in her womb. How could she expect me to soothe her, smooth it over, when he was still poisoning her. His venom shooting through my veins.

'Ed?'

The tops of her thighs, moist.

'Ed?'

Right beside me.

'Go to hell Sal.' I had tried, had given my whole self over to her and I was the one losing out.

She lay awake all through the night, rose at six, showered quickly and pulled on a pair of jeans and baggy jumper.

'Where are you going?'

'Rob's,' she answered quietly, but deadly serious. 'Aren't you going to stop me Ed? Tell me what a big mistake I'm making, what an asshole thing it is I'm about to do and that I'll regret it for the rest of my life.'

'Don't have to.'

You know what? I thought it was so funny I burst out laughing. Christ, was I roaring.

So off she ran up to Belsize Park, to the white stucco fronted house, converted into three luxury apartments, of which Rob occupied the uppermost. Sal rested a moment to catch her breath, leant against the For Sale sign staked into the grassy verge in front of the house. Selling, moving up in the world, probably investing in a home, the expectation of children jump-rushed Sal's mind. His car parked along the pavement in its usual place. She rushed up the steps to the door, the old key twisting in the lock . . .

Are you still listening Angel?

'Mmm, Sal went to Rob's . . . Wednesday morning, day Coleen called, day you killed her.' Angel's eyes close over and she snuggles close up to me.

'Yeah, you know I was thinking just now, about all this shit . . . this –'

'Shush,' mumbles Angel, 'I've heard enough. Shush.'

I rub my hands over my face and yawn loudly.

'Yeah you're right. I've said enough.'

We're sitting in the caff, waiting for Fischer, it's ten to three and Angel's dozed off.

She looks like a sleeping child, her hair all matted and shorn. Angel has short spiky hair, sticking up randomly. We met several days back, same night Fischer found us. I tripped over her, scraped her up from the ground and breathed some life into her.

She was all bloody and done in, curled into a ball, slunk beside a heap of compost. Discarded like some left-over waste and shoved out of sight. I wiped the blood from her eyes with the back of my sleeve and saw a kind of innocence and her breath was sweet. Jesus, I thought, thank you.

'Help me.'

I cradled her in close to me.

'Help me,' she whimpered.

'It'll be okay.'

She spat at me. Into my hand, a red-smeared tooth fell. I wrapped it in a handkerchief and stuffed it into my pocket.

'It will be okay, I swear.'

Then she passed out in my arms.

'Christ man, this is bad shit, man,' I thought I could hear Neville in the background. I'm not sure if he was there or not. He had been with me earlier in the evening.

The day Angel came into my life, must be almost a week ago, I had found myself back roaming the streets close to the old flat in Kentish Town, hadn't been there in over a fortnight. Neville had contacted me to say he was back from his South American trip and had a proposal to put to me. Neville was full of shit, his trip was in reality a stay in hospital, but he amused me and having no particular plans, I reckoned I'd go hang out with him.

He'd given me my own key – I'd been kipping there since the night of the culling but split when Coleen showed up with Roger and sprog, aware my face wasn't much welcome back at the block. Roger had issued a fatwa against me.

I'd told Neville I'd meet him at his, around six. I got off the tube at Camden Town and walked up Kentish Town Road, stopping off at the Arcades to kill some time, then headed off to the flats.

Practically bumped straight into Coleen. As I was crossing the courtyard, making straight for the stairwell, she had appeared at the bottom, calling Kevin in for his tea, her Glaswegian accent cutting through the frosted air.

'Kevin, your tea's ready, Kevin . . .' she blared out his name, I could see the flat's windows boarded up. Neville had helped with the finishing touches of my make-over.

I swooped down to tie an imaginary shoe lace and she hollered over to me.

'You seen a kid anywhere?'

'Saw some playing under the bridge,' diverting attention from me, the bridge being in the opposite direction. 'Wait till I get my hands on him . . . Kevin . . .' and she flat-foot plodded forward, past me. I ran up the stairs into Neville's place, let myself in. He was sitting facing the TV screen, playing *Death Wish 2* on the PlayStation.

'Hey man.' I slapped him on the shoulder.

'What you doing here?'

'You asked me over.'

He seemed agitated; I put it down to the medication he was on.

'I didn't say nothing.'

'Neville, you said you'd a proposal you wanted to discuss with me.'

'I never said nothing.'

'Well nice to see you too.' There was a carton of unopened orange juice on the counter. I pulled up a chair beside Neville and helped myself to the juice.

'How was your trip?'

'Okay.' He hadn't yet turned to face me.

'You mean you went all the way to South America and it was only okay.'

'Ed, I'm trying to play a game here, why don't you piss off.'

Someone had obviously ruffled his feathers. He turned to face me, the same someone had also cracked him one, 'cause his eye was half closed.

'What happened?'

He paused before saying, 'I dunno.'

'What? Did Mummy have to take her fist to you? Have you been a bad boy Neville?'

'Fuck off Ed.'

'Poop your pants?'

'I'm not saying anything.'

'Walk into a doorknob, did you?'

A colleague of Sal's once arrived into work with dark shades covering a bruised eye, prompting much concern, to which she replied, her slip with gravity had met with the bulbous end of a doorknob. What are the chances of that? Sal, who knew and rather liked this woman's husband, charming and funny, began, ironically as it happened, leaving self-assertion pamphlets on her desk.

'How's your mum?' I flicked Neville's earlobe and he swatted me away.

'Asleep.' No fun here I reckoned and went in search of some spliff, decided I may as well get wrecked.

'Ed, get lost. I want you to go.'

'Make me Neville.' I was feeling contrary, loved to tease him, he'd always get flappy and flustered.

'It's not my fault.'

'Neville, I never said it was.'

I snatched the controls off him. He looked up at me.

'Ed?'

'Yes.'

'I got this great new medication.'

'Oh yes.'

'Nice pills, you won't feel a thing.'

We exchanged knowing looks and from there on in, it went a little hazy.

My memory became obscured, but will come back to me eventually. Smoked out of it, and having guzzled a palmful of pills, the pair of us decided to go for a wander, a goosey-gander. Neville suggested the city farm, up off the Prince of Wales Road, past the Kentish Town baths and straight down to the end. He retained a childlike fascination with four-legged animals and would, on occasion, still chase birds.

The farm lies on a disused tract of land running alongside the railway. It has all the usual farmyard animals; chickens, roosters, horses, cows, ducks, a huge fat sow, goats and donkey rides on the weekends. Neville is a fan and it's free to the public. He loved it up there, it was a month of Sundays for him and he could be found feeding the chickens or doing the workshops, which, strictly speaking, were for the kiddies but he was tolerated as having a real empathy with the young ones. It appeared Neville also had a nocturnal fondness for sheep and had worked out a way to get into the farm, undetected, at night.

We clip-clopped up there, I piggy-backed it on Neville, who squealed in excitement till we tumbled. Leg-up over a wall, listening out for stray bleatings, and then snuck down to the far field, where some sheep lay clustered together beneath a disused bridge. By this stage both of us were flying.

There we were, prodding sheep from their woolly slumbers, Neville's fly unzipped, wielding his dick like a stick, and laughing, 'Who's a pretty girl then, silly bitch, bitch, I'm going to get her, fuck her up real bad, the bitch won't know what's coming to her, you're gonna help me.'

'You're on your own mate.' Sheep weren't my thing and Nev was going crazy, lashing out big time. He was shouting back at me, 'Stupid bitch,' running up the slope after the sheep.

Sheep clustered . . .

A shiver slid down my spine and I turned round sharply.

Three guys, hiding in the shadows, emerged out from the side of the wall, shunting Angel between them. Shady characters, I could see right through them. Motion slowed down to a fraction of time. I forgot where I was, Angel moved in balletic leaps from one to the other, the impact of blows dispersed by inert forces. She offered no resistance and danced in torpid movements, between fingers, clenched over into tight fists, and the bare brick wall. Three caricatures of broad-backed beasts with luminous eyes, and Neville and I tripping real bad. My sensory perceptions pin-point acute as every vertebrae in her back rounded over to envelope the oncoming blow. I slunk back – was this really happening? Doubted it, but it kept on, the men goading each other, taking turns, as Angel doubled over, punctured, fell, then was hoisted up like a string puppet, rag doll, pulled up, collapsed, approval bayed at every received thrust.

Bare-knuckle boxing and I had only witnessed such crude brutality as a kid, when at school a crowd of us had gathered in the corridors around these two guys pulping each other, egging them on in primitive whoops. Clapping in unison till a teacher marched down the hallway and pulled the pair apart. I didn't really look at Angel; instead, I became transfixed by the men's behaviour, their pack mentality and palpable excitement, their force united and focused on what they were doing. Little Angel hadn't the strength to retaliate. Outnumbered, she welcomed each blow. I have to admit I joined in with the hooting and cajoling so as not to become conspicuous.

Then, slumped over, she crumpled to the ground, hard boot kicks to the middle of her back, and all I could think was, where's your saviour now honey?

Angel lay still, choking up blood and the leader raised his

arms in a salute of victory. 'You fucking bitch,' and he let roar, let rip a guttural cry. The others had disappeared, perhaps there weren't any others. I can't really remember. I can't be certain.

The victor clambered up the side of the bank to the railway tracks overhead.

I remained where I was, slumped over by the side of the wall, waited till I could no longer hear his retreating footsteps, till silence descended and then I went to her aid.

'Hey, it'll be okay.'

Christ the state of her. 'I swear it'll be okay.'

'Shit, this is bad man, this is bad.' I could hear Neville's voice, somewhere out there in the darkness. Poor Neville, he was really shook up.

Later that night, much later, when things began to settle, when Angel had been stitched together and bound up, I cradled her real close, tight as can be. Then I asked her what she wished for, more than anything else in the world . . . and you know what she said, she replied,

'A heaven.'

See that's the kind of person Angel is, full of hope, and that's the precise moment I fell in love with her.

Christ, I wish Fischer would hurry up, and the rain would cease and Gloria would change the music. I yawn loudly, can feel the stretch in my jaw. Angel's snoozing beside me. Sal had become a distant memory, fading to obscurity, as Angel took her place. Funny how you can fall in love again and again. There's no such thing as one love, there's loads, maybe that's why I was so tolerant of Sal's infidelities. Sal, who I had loved to death, she wouldn't recognize me now, yet I know in my heart of hearts, she'd approve of what I was up to.

Her dying wish, the last name on her lips. 'Rob . . . Rob . . .'

I swore to get him and I will.

Sal's final utterance, 'Ob . . . ob . . .'

Heck, it sounded to me like Rob.

I cough, shift along the caff bench and ease myself up, slouch back to the kitchen area carrying the paper-thin plate.

'Gloria, were you ever on *Blind Date*?'

'What's tha . . .' She too has drowsed off, her lids shuttered over.

'Only, I noticed the picture on the wall.' I point to the photo. 'Cilla Black?'

'Nah it was the other programme she does.'

The one where she makes dreams come true. 'What she do for you?'

Gloria blinks up at the photo.

'My brother wanted to get in touch. Hadn't seen him since I was a kid.'

'That must have been nice.'

'Not particularly, he wanted to see if I had any money he could get his mitts on.'

'Shame, that's a real shame. People can be such scum,' I pause in case she wants to add anything, you know elaborate further, but she doesn't.

'Do you have any chocolate?' I suddenly get the urge for some sweetness.

'Mars, Twix or Yorkie.'

I'm a Mars man, so I take a bar and go sit back down.

Sal loved that book, it made perfect sense to her, the whole Venus trip, she underlined page after page of passages, clung to it like a bible, it became the truth for her.

The clock on the wall shows time to be touching three. Oh my, already.

Angel remains snoozing and I'm wondering how long it will take Fischer to get here, though not knowing where he's coming from makes that difficult, 'Duh!' It's all within reach now. My final wish fulfilled. After Sal had gone, my initial instinct had been to kill Rob but I dismissed it, didn't want his murder hanging on my shoulders, not that remorse was something I felt much. His death, I concluded, would be more of a punishment to those left behind. I wanted to punish him, rather than destroy him, so that he would feel something, perhaps even learn something.

The deed in hand has been coldly contrived. I have laboured these last six weeks over what exactly I should do, how best to extract vengeance, and I choose my words wisely, for it is a justifiable retribution. Why seek revenge, if it's only to bolster my own conceit? Now that would be a waste of five grand. All the money I have in the world, and to give half to Fischer would be ludicrous were it not a necessity. A plan conceived that would exorcise my own hatred towards Rob yet at the same time castigate this man who has ruined my life. I don't say this lightly because Sal was my life. She was everything to me.

The last of the happy times with Sal was spent up at Kenwood House, late last summer, a blissful evening listening to Vivaldi, played by some youth orchestra on the other side of the lake. The heat that day had been stifling and Sal had spent the morning moping around the flat. She'd called friends only to be told they all had plans or boyfriends or a life and Sal had found herself at a loose end. Frank had been keeping her on her toes and for the past couple of weeks Sal had worked late, on unpaid overtime. I didn't empathize, pained by the knowledge that

Frank's greasy paws had been mauling her at any given opportunity. Sal would say to me, it's just the way he is, forget it Ed, it's kinda part of the job, there's no mal-intent. Sure, whatever you say Sal, though I knew she'd end up screwing him.

That sunny morning she moaned at me, 'I want a garden to lie out in, a pool to dip my toes in, forget I'm in the city, and where no one can pester me.' I waved an old Speedo swimsuit in her face, the only one she had, which had lost its elasticity and suggested a trip to the Women's Pond up at Hampstead Heath.

I watched as she tottered off. On the way she stopped at a patisserie to buy a filled baguette and a pastry which she munched on as she hauled herself up through the fields. She was looking good, well better than she had in the past while, wearing a wraparound skirt and a t-shirt, a sweater stuffed in her trendy backpack, shades across her eyes and her hair scraped back into a ponytail. She got there just after midday, when the morning crew were packing up and the afternoon crowd, the serious sunbathers, arrive. The banks semi-circling the pond were already heaving with a various abundance of bodies and lurid towels, the grass barely showing through, so she had to pick her way over limbs and torsos to claim a spot. The temperature in the thirties, the smell of perfumed sun lotions drifting by on a light breeze with smatterings of conversation, Sal went belly down, her book open in front of her, half reading and half listening to the ceaseless chatter of womanhood. Between times, she took dips to cool down her body, then returned to her ear-marked bestseller. The afternoon rolled forward and she ended up talking to a couple of Spanish au pairs who said they were meeting friends up at Kenwood and she could hang with them if she wanted. I met up with them later.

'This is the life eh?' she smiled.

'See Sal, things will happen if you let them.'

The sun began to set and music swirled through the air in gusts, the first of the fireworks sent soaring upward.

'Ed, shut up, let me enjoy the moment.'

'I was only trying to . . .'

'Ed, hush.' We lay back on a tartan rug, surrounded by loud Spanish chatter and laughter.

'Mm, yes, this is the life.'

Suppose now for a moment you could do whatever you wanted. There were no unsurmountable boundaries. Your moral conscience dissolved and though your actions would inevitably create repercussions, you had no fear or emotional attachment that would hinder anything you did. A situation whereby you can have whatever you want, do whatever, be whatever, the worst you can ever do has already been done.

Of course I'm talking about myself. My post-Sal self, what happened after the event took place. What I've actually been up to, in these last six weeks.

It felt like a freedom only money could buy. The jackpot flashing, winning numbers called, horse comes in, chest imploding as a zillion tensions hissed from every pore. Sally Jane Edwards is:

a) gone

b) over

c) no more

d) dead

Ehh . . .

*

Neville for chrissakes, call a friend, ask the audience, you dimwit. Duh, time's run out and he got it wrong.

'It was a trick question.'

'Man it was so damn obvious.'

I don't know anything. I know everything. I made a suggestion.

'Roll another spliff.'

So back to Wednesday, the night I killed Sal.

In Neville's grimy front room, two people were lost in their own silence, Sal lying fresh in death and it must have been about four in the morning. I had eased myself into a vertical position. It was time to go, certain there was a mountain of stuff I should be doing, the destruction of Sal's effects for one being a principal priority.

'Neville . . .' The rest of the sentence had backlogged somewhere in my mind.

No response was forthcoming.

'Nev, the flat, I'm going back down . . .'

'Huh.'

'See you tomorrow?'

'Aghh.' Slumped in the beanbag, dribble running down the side of his mouth. Neville had reached his own personal nirvana.

'Thanks for the smoke.'

'Mmmm.'

I let myself out and slumped downstairs, back to our flat. Pushed the key in the door, wondering what I'd find, if I'd imagined the whole scenario and Sal would be there, asleep in the bed, curled up dreaming. The door creaked ajar and I shuffled inside, all the lights switched off in case I saw something I didn't want to see. Softly, I called out her name through the darkness. 'Are you there Sal?' Testing the silence.

I suspect the first thing a criminal does is return to the scene of the crime, check nothing has changed, everything left just so.

Sal wasn't there. I'd succeeded, finally dumped her, black refuse sacked and chucked out, past her sell by date, her best before long gone. She must have put on at least a stone in the last year. Sal . . . and the bed was empty, no more hogging of the duvet, warm toes and plump belly, her hair spread out over the pillow and reassuring voice, 'Gee Ed, I had like the worst nightmare ever, like I was possessed and my body invaded and it was you Ed.'

She didn't appear as an apparition, all forgiving, 'Hey, don't worry Ed, we all make mistakes, I'm only dead. It was my fault as much as yours. Look, let's put the past behind us . . . right? We'll call it quits and start over, only I won't be there. You really are better off by yourself, though you didn't have to be so rough. Ed, I know, I bear the brunt of the blame and I can see where you were coming from, I mean from your position there wasn't really any other alternative. So I forgive you, Ed . . . Ed, are you listening?'

I couldn't hear a thing. Goddamn it woman, why did you have to push me so far. Why make me the villain? I should have tried harder, should have been stronger, should have picked up on all those little things, your squeaks for help. Shit when I look back now, it's easy to see, it's clear still water, abc building blocks. Should have gone about things differently. Everyone needs a little help from time to time and I needn't have been so hard on her.

'Sal, I truly loved you, I remember your weary eyes, heavy breath before your soul extinguished. Sal, I never meant to hurt you.'

'No one ever does Ed. I understand. It was time to move on.'

'It was too easy to kill you Sal. You egged me on, begged me for release.'

'You're on your own now Ed.'

Caught a glimpse of my reflection, obscured by the shadowy gloom in the freestanding bedroom mirror. A reflective glass bought at Greenwich market on a Sunday, during Sal's 'Rob period', so they could watch themselves fuck.

Made me want to kill her all over again; instinctively my hand reached out for the weapon resting on top of the chest of drawers next to Sal's monthly Travelcard. A pair of scissors, sharp and effective. Who'd have thought a pair of scissors could be so deadly.

You know what? I wanted to continue our war. Nothing was over, it had all just begun. I required stoking, the momentum from what had happened must be contained and put to good use. The initial flood of energy had petered out to a trickle. I was exhausted, fell back upon the bed and rested on plumped-up pillows. The hard-backed edges of Sal's diary prodded me in the ribs, she had just finished writing in it, when I had gone for her.

Sal's dirge, her diary. Read me, it screamed, validate action taken.

Sal's life, as perceived by Sal: a record kept from the age of ten to the present day. Her final entry being the whole Coleen scenario. Her very last words: 'Something's going to give and I have a feeling it's going to be me . . . when is this ever going to end????? My fucking head is splitting.' Sal was always prone to hyperbole.

And there it ended. Hadn't I done her a favour and answered her final plea?

The book, trendy weirdy paper, handmade by some Indian peasant woman on the banks of the holy Ganges.

Heavy lidded on the bed, spread over the mock Liberty patterned quilt, I lay back and wondered what else Sal could have kept from me. What secrets lay hidden within? Must I release them all?

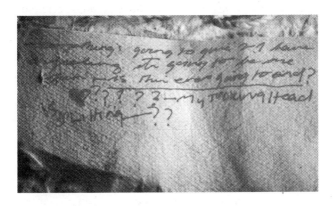

Sal's final entry, strictly speaking it had been Rob

Of course, her thoughts were public property now, especially those besmirching details. To avoid suspicion, I could rewrite her history, if needs be, now there was a thought . . .

Perhaps something along the lines of:

'I wait for death to quash my suffering . . .' Nah, too dramatic even for Sal.

'I feel like death, things aren't going so good for me at the moment . . .' Too flippant.

'Black, black despair, sleep, sleep spare me, dear God sweet salvation . . .' Mmmm possible.

'Won loads of money and have disappeared . . .' Now you're talking.

The bedside lamp switched on, my eyes smarting in the glare as I eased her diary open. So much to take in, all naked as she bled over the pages. The paper soaked in her thoughts and I began to read. I flicked through the mundane crap, all her messy female feelings, her aches and yearnings and feminine hygiene problems. Pages brimming with banalities: *had a flirt with the fishmonger today/ Patel remarked on my new haircut/ work's a drag but am going out tonight/ Rob called by, I think I'm still in love with him/ wondering whether I should ask for a pay rise?/ passed by a building site today and a guy said, Cheer up love, it's not the end of the world. Must remember to smile.*

Stuffed full of such drivel, it was almost too pathetic to read. When I came upon the following three pages.

Couldn't face writing for the past few weeks, finding it hard to even look in the mirror, everything's a total mess. I bumped into Rob at a club, he couldn't talk, had to get back to his new girlfriend, told me they were living together. Already? He's only known her five seconds and may as well have stabbed me a thousand times . . . et tu? Redredging everything and it hurts like hell, I mean, only last week he called by for a bj, saying how he'd loved the way I gave head. This whole continuing Rob saga, why can't he see we made such a good team, we were strong together, I just don't get it. Thought things would improve when Petra set me up on a couple of blind dates, the first was a funny guy with a heavy moustache who kept on about anal sex and was I into it, in short, an asshole; the other one was more the traditional type, he went into great detail about his ex-girlfriend's foibles and how he would never trust another woman after finding her in bed with his brother. To top it all off, he even got my name wrong at the end of the meal and called me Jane! Then I lost my bag or it was nicked, filofax, credit cards, the works. I'd bought myself some new Mac makeup for a treat and all of it lost. Most probably stolen, can't be certain, cos I was in such a daze the day it happened (the morning after seeing Rob) and I thought I'd treat myself to some retail therapy, so there I was in Selfridges trying on a sweet Mui Mui dress that I couldn't afford and that didn't fit. Can't believe it but I've gone up a whole dress size. Afterwards in a cafe, I went to pay and couldn't find my bag!! Had to spend the next four hours trying to cancel all my cards. Next shitty thing to happen was on the way to work. I fell down some steps in the tube station, cos some bastard had pushed me aside, saying 'Look where you're going love' and no one came to help. I tumbled down three steps, my skirt ending up round my arse, exposing my rear and on the blob, I had leaked and there was a big stain on my knickers and some schoolboys burst out laughing. Later that afternoon I broke down in the office, literally burst out crying. The photocopier had jammed up, for like the nth time, and Frank lost his rag, called me an imbecile in front of the whole office. Nothing is going my way, like zero in my life, that's it, my whole life is one big zero, my aura has gone off and is stinking . . .

She did go on, consistently ranting for another page and a half, tedious self-indulgence about how awful everything was; note I'm not mentioned, the one and only positive thing in her life, bypassed.

It continued, the handwriting getting smaller, tiny letters, as if that would somehow make her next confession less extreme.

So afterwards everyone in the office was being really kind, Frank especially and he took me out to dinner to make up for it, the Groucho club, as if rubbing shoulders with London's media crew would lift my spirits. We got drunk, very drunk. Ended up telling Frank everything, the whole Rob deal, and Frank was really sweet, saying things like he thought I was being too hard on myself and that I had a load of talent and that I was beautiful (yeah right!) and it was strange, cos I saw another side to him, behind the despot veneer he parades round the office. Usually he's such a twerp but he began telling me about all the pressures he had to deal with in his life and how his wife was a manic depressive. Apparently she's been institutionalized loads and the marriage dead for years, that's why he fucks round all the time, but he still loves her and the kids. He'd never leave her, he can't and he told me how trapped he felt and how expensive private health was, not to mention the boarding school fees for the children, etc. He really opened up and for

the first time I saw Frank as being vulnerable. I
realized it must be tough for him, and that everyone
had troubles and it sort of made me feel less bad
about my own situation, I know that sounds weird
but it's true.

We hugged each other at the end of the night, and
it was nice. I mean I'd never thought of Frank in
sexual terms, never, I swear, but then the next day at
work, it was like we crossed some barrier, having
confided in each other.

Anyhow, our latest commission has been this
documentary soap about people who work in sewers,
like who in their right mind would want to watch
such drivel. We, F and I, have been trawling through
potential shitmongers, hoping to unearth a rough
diamond, like one who's really an opera singer or
scientist or even vaguely interesting.

Been working my ass off, as per usual, late every
night, and I suppose Frank and I have been getting on
really well, laughing at all the sad blokes we've come
across and we end up grabbing something to eat at
the end of the day, or going for a drink and talking till
all hours. The deadline was last night.

Yeah, yeah, yeah and you can guess where this is leading . . . so let's skip, skip, skip, to the loo my Darlin' . . . I
can't bear anymore of Sal's excuses, excuses for what she
did next.

The office was empty, we'd finished the second bottle
of champagne and the Thai we'd sent out for. My
breath was garlicky and I was totally smashed. Frank

had booked a taxi to take me home and I suppose we had been flirting heavily, but I thought it was just flirting and he was going on about love and the need to express yourself and how sexy he considered me, that I'd a beautiful body, saying stuff like, you should just let yourself go, be a little crazy, do the unexpected, then saying how I came across a little uptight at times and how men found it offputting, that I should loosen up a little, not take things so seriously . . . We ended up on the sofa in reception, doing it . . . Christ . . . I regretted it immediately. I mean what if he expects more, what if I lose my job. I am <u>so</u> weirded out, I can't tell you and like he has a really short squat dick and didn't use anything, so I've had to go to the doctor today to get the morning after pill. Maybe I led him on, I'm not sure. I swear I didn't intend it, it was a huge mistake, grosses me out just thinking about it.

Me too. Reading that filth made me feel dog dirty. The lying stupid bitch that Sal was; I'd always had an inkling she'd fucked Frank, she'd neither denied nor admitted it. How in God's name, I'll never understand. Was she reeking of desperation? Was that it? Succumbing to flattery and believing all that crap about Frank's wife. He used her, she let him.

I closed my eyes, sunk back down on the bed and switched off the lamp.

I could hear my heart beating. Imagine how reading that made me feel.

Actually, it reconfirmed everything, the necessity of getting rid of Sal.

It was definitely the right thing to do.

As for Frank, he really should have known better and I thought it would be fun to get back at him. Yeah there was definite potential to have a little fun.

As it later transpired, twelve grand's worth.

Felled by sleep with dreams, doubt ridden that I hadn't finished Sal off properly and she was still breathing. Swathed in her nightie, the Marks and Spencer's comfortable one, brush cotton, which made her look like a granny and at the same time reminded her of childhood. She floated above me, her hair fallen over her face, disguising her expression but she was moaning, 'I'm not dead, help me, help me Ed.' I lay directly below, my arms instinctively reaching up to throttle her, her neck cold, tightening my clasp around it, wringing it tight so that my fingers met to intertwine. Her neck shrunk within my clutches, her head hung lower, distended, drooping down, our noses touching and I could feel the weakest of breath . . . Ed . . . Ed . . .

'Wake up Ed . . . Ed . . . Ed . . .'

Neville was at the door, rapping hard. I jolted upright, my senses coming a slow second, the diary sent flying off my chest and landing on the rug by the bed.

'I'm coming, I'm coming.' My lips shaped the words.

'Ed, you up?'

'Give me a minute.'

My legs swung over the side of the bed, clashing with the ground. Each and every sensory motion heightened as if for the first time. The coarse wool of the bedroom rug brushing against my toes, the weight of my upper torso, the movement of each step, the lightness of my head finding balance on the top of my spine. A grin extended over my lips. The pounding fist against the surface of the front door.

'I'm coming.' The sound of my voice reverberated sharply in my ears as if standing next to a screeching set of speakers.

For a split second I had no memory of what had occurred the night before. I was innocent. Nothing happened till my eyes stretched open and a host of recollections flew out like sharp dart arrows.

'I'm coming,' I yelled out to Neville.

I unlatched the door, letting it swing wide. Neville was dressed in tracksuit bottoms and a sweat shirt.

'What time is it?' I asked.

'Around three p.m. I think,' Neville replied, hesitantly.

I'd slept half the day away. It was Thursday, Coleen's henchman Roger expected anytime.

'What do you want?'

'You mentioned you were doing some DIY.'

Had I and what else had I told him?

'Not now Neville, I have to think.'

'Can I come in?'

'No.'

'Why?'

'Just no, okay. I'll see you later.' He looked at me forlornly.

'Look, I have important stuff to do.'

I shut the door, then peered through the spyhole. He was still there, with a hangdog expression on his face.

Kickstarted into motion, I turned towards the kitchen to put on a pot of coffee, forgetting I'd already decimated the place. I don't function so well without coffee, a consideration I'd failed to take into account the night before. My head teeming, first thing was to get rid of all Sal's stuff, erase every-thing of her, of us and leave the flat in a befitting state of welcome for the return of Coleen. That was the order of the day, it all came back to me.

Neville's name ricocheted from the tip of my tongue outward. I ran to the door. I'd need help and his would be as good as anybody's. He was still there, stuck on *pause*.

'You definitely said something about DIY,' his tone sounding accusatory.

'Yeah sure. Look, are you hungry? Would you do me a favour?' I sent him packing with a crisp tenner to buy some coffee and sandwiches.

'And bring back the change.'

Off he went while I pondered; everything had to go, TV, stereo, microwave, cuddly toys, windows, curtains, rugs, light fittings. Late afternoon, the light already fading. My fingers clicking as I paced through the flat taking a mental inventory.

Twenty minutes later Neville arrived back with fish and chips and cans of Coke and a huge fat bloke named Jonno. No coffee.

'Listen guys, I got to move out today.' I pointed to all the furniture. 'It's all got to be shifted.'

'Where's it going?' Neville posed a serious question.

'Yours Neville. It's all going up to yours.'

'Ehh, but Ed . . . I . . .'

'Regard it as my present to you. Yeah for being such a good mate, through thick and thin.' I slapped him heartily on the shoulder. He was stunned with gratitude.

'Mum's going to be thrilled. No one ever's given me nuffin'.'

I gave him a hug. 'Listen Neville can I stay with you for a while?'

'Never had a best friend before.'

'Yeah sure, and I'll want your room.'

'Okay Ed.'

Jonno asked what was in it for him.

'A Sony TV and digital radio alarm clock?'

'Sounds okay to me.'

The next few hours were spent emptying Sal's remains, all her accumulated dross and dragging it upstairs to Neville's, the bed, sofa, armchair, bookcase, sheets, towels, towel rail, pictures, the lot. What we couldn't shift we altered; poured cement down the drains, toilet, sinks, every plughole filled. An inspired idea of mine. Then extended the same principle to the windows, nailing them shut, so that they would have to be unhinged and replaced.

We acquired a rhythm of devastation: deplete, destroy, destruct, with ant army effectiveness, listening to Haydn on the cd player. Deplete, destroy, destruct, busy workers and we were soon on top of it.

It had gone seven before I had a chance to stand still and enjoy the fruits of our handiwork. I dismissed Neville and Jonno, emptied the contents of Sal's wallet and sent them off for a curry or whatever their hearts desired. Alone, I breathed a sigh of relief in Sal's empty, unrecognizable flat. As far as I was concerned Coleen was welcome to it.

There remained nothing but a few articles of sentimental value and the phone.

It felt good to be starting afresh. Nothing lasts forever, eh Sal. Where are you now? My sweet sad Sal. The sweet sweaty smell of perspiration, my own, inveigled it's way up my nostrils and I took a final shower, letting the water flood over the floor. Wet and hollering at the top of my voice, *lah-di-lah*, how good life is, as the water pelted down cleansing my sins, before raising the hammer to the frosted glass sides. Hey, the shower unit had cost a fortune, it had taken Sal months of savings and a loan from her parents.

I didn't hear the phone ring, it was only after I'd changed and was about to unplug it, that the thought occurred to check for any missed messages.

There were four, three from Frank sounding increasingly pissed off, where are you Sal? Why haven't you rung in? What's up? His sleazy voice disgusting to me, that his tongue should have been in her mouth, the thought of his sweat and fluids and . . .

The final message was from Coleen.

'Hi Sal,' surprisingly conciliatory in tone. 'Look we're sorry and you were right.' But of course. 'Well the thing is, I really don't think it's a good idea to inform the council so Roger and I have decided you can keep the flat for another two weeks, three at the most. I'm sorry about yesterday, can you call me back when you get this message? Thanks Sal.'

How big of her, how decidedly generous of spirit, but alas, too late. I was in charge now and the flat was in pig state. It would take quite a wad of dosh to make it inhabitable again. Not a place to bring up young kids.

I gathered up the box containing Sal's nick nacks, the diary, her new filofax, credit cards, keys and bank details, almost ready to leave the past behind. My final feat to dismantle the fusebox next to the front door and what should I find sticking out of it but a heavy cream envelope, a wedding invitation, no less. I stuffed it in with the rest of Sal's effects to read later.

Unmodernized the fusebox was easy to wreck, mains turned off, then smashed. As I left the flat, I was struck by the thought of all the unpaid bills and who was going to pick them up. No longer my problem. I carried the box up to

Neville's and collapsed down on Sal's sofa, as it happened, in time to catch the final minutes of *Emmerdale* before I crashed out.

A finger prods me in the upper arm. I struggle to swat it away but its stabbing continues accompanied by a high-pitched voice.

'Oi you, wake up.'

Must have dozed off, ahh where am I?

'Oi.'

Pulling myself back to consciousness. The invitation. Ahhh man . . . I was so tired, what time is it?

Angel, whaaa? . . .

'Sleepin' beauty.'

Jesus give me strength, my eyes scrunched together, the pills worn off and I can feel the beginning of a migraine. All of Murphy's men are busy at work digging a road across my forehead. Bolting forward, the money, my money, my warm lap. My warm empty lap. Oh man, the money.

'Money,' I gasp wrenching open my eyes. 'Money,' I might be shouting this. The lights sting, I jump forward only to be hemmed in by the table top.

'Shit Christ . . .'

I'm staring straight into a face. I know that face. It's Gloria's face.

Gloria, the caff, in the caff waiting I am . . . where the fuck is my money?

'What you on about?' Gloria backs away, as if my actions are somehow threatening.

'My mo . . . my bag, where's my bag?' I'm mumbling incoherently, dazed, screwing my eyes tight to open them all the wider. Down beneath the table, fumbling around on my knees. There it is. My trusty black backpack. Must have slipped from my lap, tumbled off. It's okay, all there, safe and sound just as I'd left it, I unzip it, rummage within the contents, everything there, the two large padded envelopes in a small plastic drawstring bag. Sealed envelopes to avoid spillage. I'd taken precautions.

Here baggy bag, there's a good bag, nice bag come to Eddy, Ahhh, sweet! Pointing my finger, syrupy voice shifting to decidedly vicious. 'Don't never do that again.' Give that bag a good shaking, stuff it inside my jacket, and 'You ain't coming out till I tell you, got it?' Zip that jacket up, pat my bulging front. You can't take your eyes off things for a second these days, got to be on alert 24–7, what with the sort of characters roaming our streets. Remember Sal's bag? Stolen in broad daylight, right in front of her nose. Jesus H what am I mumbling on about?

'It's okay.' I announce this loudly, as if I have a huge audience.

The truth lies three foot away in the form of Gloria.

'Are you on drugs?' she asks.

Must have fallen into a deep state of slumber. Rubbing my hand across my face. I ache all over, sore, twist my neck from side to side, till it cracks.

'Drugs?' I reiterate, though it sounds like I'm asking for some, 'No.' Most emphatic, too emphatic.

Gloria stares across at me.

'Are you in trouble, I don't want any trouble.'

I sneeze loudly and she shrinks back disgusted, must have caught a cold, out in all weathers trying to find this place. And if I've told Angel once, I've told her a thousand times.

'Sorry, must have dropped off.'

Christ, what time is it and where the hell is Fischer?

Gloria continues to stare, like I have two heads.

I glance up at the wall clock. It could be anytime, for all I know days could have passed. I yawn loudly, trying to shrug myself awake. It's quarter past three. Christ I've only been asleep for fifteen minutes.

Where in the name of God is Fischer?

'Do you do espresso Gloria?'

She throws me a filthy look and snatches the empty can of Pepsi from the table top. 'A coffee is it?'

'That would be nice. Sorry if I gave you a fright.'

Gloria has the hump. I hope for another customer to arrive and distract her ever-growing curiosity. She knows something's up, things aren't quite right.

When she goes back behind the counter, she takes out her mobile and makes a call. Who knows what her imagination is stewing up. I'd jumped up screaming, 'Money, where's the money?' re-enacting a crime. Is she phoning the police, is that it? I mean that's all we need, a complication like that will really screw things up. Straining to catch what she's saying, her back turned to me, spinning round on her feet, 'Right, see you in a bit,' and her conversation ends. Too informal for a plea, though I'm going to have to say something. I dig my little finger into my earhole to tweak my brain in gear.

'Ed, take it easy.' Angel had woken up.

'She's on to us Angel.'

'Don't go getting paranoid Ed.'

Me paranoid? I lean back in against the bench seat and laugh out loud.

'Oi what's your problem?' Gloria sounds more in control.

Must remember to act normal.

'Angel, I have an inkling Gloria's uncomfortable in our presence, my instinct tells me she's gonna call the police.

It'll mess things up. Maybe we should wait for Fischer outside.'

'Ed, it's pouring.'

'I don't care. I don't want anything to go wrong. Not tonight.'

'I'm not going out.'

Angel can be real stubborn when she wants to.

I glance across to Gloria, feel she requires an explanation of sorts, before she draws the wrong conclusion. My main fear being the police will be called.

'So, sweet talker, what should I say?'

Angel's thinking, 'Something like,' she paused, 'something like . . . I know, sorry if you appear odd but you've just returned from abroad.'

'Bravo . . . may as well announce myself as an escaped convict. Angel, do I have to do everything in this relationship, be responsible for everything?' I'm getting agitated.

'Relax, Ed. I'll do it okay? I'll explain the situation and everything will be fine.'

'Yeah, yeah, yeah.'

'Don't you trust me?'

Trust, now there's a mighty word. I should never have trusted Sal, she betrayed me big time but you know what? I've moved on from those days. Angel is different, she is better, much better for me.

Gloria meets my stare and flinches, misses the mug and pours some boiling water over the counter. I look away. Where in the name of God was Fischer?

Angel winks, 'We were mugged, that's why we're in this state. Got it, and that's why you're so jumpy.' So close to the truth it sounds plausible.

A finger gently taps the side of my nose.

'Now you're talking, sweet Angel.'

I believe in angels . . . I tune back into Gloria's melody maker, the sound waves of Abba, lead vocal Frida. Sal adored Abba as a teenager and then again when they came back into retro fashion. *I'll cross the stream, I have a dream* . . . Yeah that's exactly what happened, the ferryman took Sal across to the other side. See Sal had this dream and it shattered and blew her to pieces.

I dig my hand down into my pockets in search of loose change, money for my Angel, a fiver pulled from the folds of a familiar cream-coloured card and twiddled in my thumbs.

Gloria stamps the mug down on the counter top. 'Your coffee's ready.'

'Go to it girl, appease our Gloria. I'd only come across too aggressive.'

Angel gets up. 'You do trust me, don't you Ed?'

'Sure I do.'

' 'Cause we're in this together.'

'I know.'

'You need me as much as I do you.'

I let her take control of the situation.

She walks towards the counter.

She'll come up good when the bruising subsides, will Angel. When all of this is over and Rob has been dealt with, she'll sparkle. The night I found her, when she wished for a heaven, she was nothing more than a whisper, the softest of presences. 'I'll help you,' she pledged, moving into me.

'Whatever happens now, we're in it together Ed.'

Angel's said she's going to grow her hair, she'll let it grow long and curly and has promised to take good care of it. It's short and stubby, sticking up all over the place, all wrong, and she bought these little girly clips to try and make it appear a bit neater. It looks funny, her bruised face and plastic flowers dotted through her hair. It's all the rage she told me, pop stars wear them. For my part I've promised to buy her some nice clothes, she looks like a ragged street bum. When Sal was younger she went through a phase of wearing hats. Her favourite place was a hat shop up the lane from St Christopher's Place, off Oxford Street. The name of it I can't recall but she'd bought herself a black leather cap, slightly too big, so that the peak fell to the side of her head and she resembled a Chaplinesque urchin, whereas Angel, well she just looks rough and weary.

Gloria pushes the mug towards her.

Angel hands over the fiver, 'Do you have any change?'

Gloria shuffles back a pace or two, towards her moneybox and lifts the lid, she takes out a handful of coins.

'Thanks.' In return, Angel offers her up the best smile she can muster. 'Look I'm sorry if I seem a bit on edge, a couple of days back I was mugged and . . .'

Angel's eyes cast downward, as if ashamed of herself.

Gloria shrugs her shoulders. 'No offence but we don't cater to the public as a general rule. Boris had no right arranging to meet you here.'

It's clear she wants rid of us as soon as possible, looking up at the clock, counting the change out into Angel's palm.

It's three twenty-five.

'When did he say he was coming?'

'Should have been here already.' Angel apologizes for our continued presence. 'I'll call, check where he is.'

Angel comes back to me.

'Ed, you better ring Fischer.'

Feel like deducting money for lateness and then notice three missed messages, all from Fischer. Must have called when I was snoozing, lulled by the mobile's vibrations. I didn't bother to retrieve them. I punch in his numbers and wait for an answer.

'Fischer,' I yell, loud enough for Gloria to hear, to show her I'm being proactive.

'Ed, where you are?'

Excuse me, now that's rich coming from him. 'Where the hell are you?'

I'm expecting his reply to be a hazy apology, weather delayed, on his way. Nothing is to impede our plan and then he says to me, 'I have accident.'

'What's that. The line's cracking up.' Tell me I'm not hearing what I'm hearing.

'Ed, I have accident.'

'You're joking me.'

'No.'

'Angel, he's had a fucking accident.'

'What?'

'You git . . . you utter idiot . . .' an inner blare of vitriol flashes from my temples. What has to be done, has to be done today. We've been through the plan a billion times. Without him I can't proceed. I can't bear to listen to this. Angel takes over the handset.

'Fischer?'

'Angel, I sorry, don't worry, we still do it.'

Sorry ain't good enough . . .

'What happened?' she asks. Assess the damage, good starting point Angel, I could kill him, throttle him.

'A car jam into mine, car complete goner.'

I knew it, he's a lunatic driver, the guy is a friggin loon behind the wheel, hasn't a clue what he's doing.

'Not my fault.' And a liar. Fischer is undoubtedly a lying shit. I don't give a toss whose fault it is, just tell me the job's still on.

'I have small concussion and leg need brace but I okay.' He's obviously a little shook up, poor fuckwit Fischer, hands a little shaky are they? all the better to cut with.

I can't think straight.

'Where are you?'

'Hospital.'

'Which one?'

'St Mary's. I have seen no one yet.'

'How long have you been there?'

'Two hour.'

'We'll come get you.'

'Car is complete goner.'

'Yeah you said.'

'I okay, we still do it.'

'Jesus Fischer . . .'

Already I'm thinking, a hospital is a good place to pick up a doctor.

You know I'd specifically asked him not to work, I'd said, take this night off, tomorrow you'll be rich, well a richer man than you are at present. What difference does one night make? So what does he do? I just don't get it, he has to go jeopardize the whole arrangement. He'd promised to drive some feeble old dame out to Heathrow, some heap of rattling bones whose whole life now revolved around her Scottish Terrier. He'd said to me, 'Promise is promise, she like mother to me since one day.' My heart bleeds . . .

'I swear I won't let you down?' He already has.

Six weeks in the making, and livid I switch the mobile off, my face set in anger.

Angel giggles nervously.

I swing round to face Gloria. 'He's only gone and had an accident.'

'Boris . . . Is he okay?'

'He's in hospital.'

'Why are you laughing. It's not funny.'

On the contrary, it's actually hysterical. Part of me wants to cry, the other scream. This, I hadn't envisaged. It isn't accounted for. Doesn't figure in the sums. There's no way I'll give up, do the job myself, if I have to. You can't rely on anyone but yourself.

'Angel don't look at me like that.'

'Well, it could have happened to anyone,' she says.

'Why do you have be so philosophical all the time?'

She shrugs a shoulder. 'It's happened, *un fait accompli*.' So the girl speaks French.

My face is curtained by my hands for some quick reassessments.

Plan A abandoned, or rather, altered. Yes I prefer that, yes a slight alteration, that sounds even better and we'll go and collect Fischer. No big deal, everything's under control. St Mary's isn't too far from Belsize Park. We are redeeming the situation. A little time has been lost, an hour at the most, the remaining challenge (positive word, *challenge*, I like it) being transport. Surmountable. We're in a cabbies' caff, one is bound to show up soon.

Yeah . . . let's keep things in perspective. Fischer was involved in a car accident. He's had an accident. All is not lost.

Stop fidgeting Angel.

All fingers and thumbs, I'm getting cold and shivery.

The card has been shredded. Torn to pieces in the plastic ashtray. The wedding invitation which has been on my person these last six weeks has finally met its end.

Jane and Peter Brookman have great pleasure inviting Sal,
plus 1, to celebrate the marriage of their daughter Justine
to Rob, son of Joan and Dominic Felpps, on Thursday
14th February 2002, at Camden Registry Office, ceremony
12 noon and afterwards at the Landmark Hotel,
lounge suit, reception 12.30 p.m. followed by lunch.
RSVP

It's just gone 3.35 a.m. on Thursday 14th February and Rob is due to be getting married later today. There remains a limited number of hours in which to carry out my slightly warped but deliciously succinct act of vengeance, in memory of Sal and for my own sweet satisfaction.

If Sal were alive, she would have resorted to tradition. She would have made a pathetic sight, stood at the registry office. Yep, I can see her dressed in her finery, she'd have bought a new outfit, made such an effort and stuffed her bag with tissues. Overcome with emotion, she'd have watched as Rob committed to some other cow and then she'd have broken, a final twist in her guts, snapping. One for dramatics, Sal would have excelled in the situation. I can hear her voice, the beseeching and pitiful whine. Attempting to steal the spotlight, she would have intervened at that crucial point – 'if there is any objection to this marriage, speak now, or forever . . . forever hold your peace'. And she would have cried out, *Oh, oh . . . it should have been me. Oh yeah, it should have been me, somebody call the po'lice that woman down there is a doggone thief . . .*

Another top tune from Sal's favourite 100, Yvonne Fair – *Motown Hits of Gold*, Vol. 7.

I could imagine Sal flinging herself towards him, in a sad, last desperate bid. She'd have been laughed at, humiliated in front of the whole congregation, then thrown out.

Me? Well I'm going for the more sophisticated approach.

'Ed, snap out of it.'

'You're right Angel, it ain't over till it's over.'

'Yeah, get it together.'

It's gone all quiet and I realize Gloria has switched the radio off.

'Time to go,' she shouts.

And she's right, got to make a move now. Got to get to Paddington. Transport and we'd be needing some.

'Gloria what are the chances of getting a cab at this time of night?'

'You'd be lucky.'

Stuck in the bog end of the city, edging towards four and my mind is racing.

'You don't reckon someone will come by?'

'Nah, not now.' She's been in this business a long time and I take her at her word.

'Shit Angel, we're stuck.' Gloria is switching off all her kitchen appliances, she empties the moneybox, opens her purse and pushes the notes in.

'It's time to go, I'm shutting up.'

'We've got to get to Paddington.'

'No point looking at me,' she says, taking her padded leather jacket off a wall hook.

'You right?' She says egging us out as fast as possible and the last thing she wants is trouble.

'Gloria how are you getting home?'

'That's no concern of yours.'

Oh but it is and she has a nose for trouble. I take in a deep sniff.

'Look,' I start by reasoning with her. 'The thing is, we're in a bit of a fix, we've got to get to Paddington and need help. How are you getting home?' All I want her to do is give me a straight answer.

'I can't help, I've to get home myself.' She zips up her jacket. There's a bike helmet on the hook to the left of her and it suddenly makes sense, she'd be a bit of a biker what with her hidden tattoos, bleached hair and hardline exterior. Perfect, exactly what's required in the situation.

'Gloria I'll pay you, whatever you want.' See, even under extreme pressure, I am a reasonable person.

She eyes us up and down, 'cause we look like we haven't two coins to rub together.

'How much do you want?'

'I want you out of here now. If you don't mind.'

But I do mind, we'd to get to the hospital, where Fischer is languishing in pain. It's an emergency.

'Gloria, I'm in an emergency situation.'

'Anymore of your bullshit and I'm calling the police.' Touchy and she means it too, as she goes towards the phone.

'There's no need for that, I just want a way out of here.' I move towards her slow and deliberate.

'That's it, I'm calling the police.'

Oh Gloria why did you have to go and say that?

I do my best to discourage her and plead, 'Name your price woman, whatever you want.'

But from the beginning she thought we were trouble and now she's lifted up the receiver.

There was nothing else for it. I'll have to take out the gun Neville gave me.

Did you honestly think a person like myself would wander these mean streets without one? He gave it to me by way of an apology.

'Ed, you got to be careful.'

'You total dick.'

I recently paid poor Neville a little visit, and just to set the record straight I said to him, 'I should kill you Neville.' Tied him to a chair and began taunting him.

'But we're friends Ed.' Had he forgotten the night of the fight?

'You sad fuck traitor.' And he'd shat his pants, scared I'd actually do something horrible. I hovered over him, circled him, like he was prey.

He offered me everything he had, which amounted to sweet FA, then announced, 'Okay take my gun.' He'd mentioned it once or twice before, his drug dealer had left it with him before he went away to spend some time courtesy of Her Majesty. Neville had it wrapped up in cloth, hidden in his mother's room, stuffed into one of the teddy bears resting on the pillow. Now that would come in useful.

'It's not loaded,' he squealed, as I shoved it up to the side of his head.

'Are you sure?'

I pulled back the trigger and pop.

'Yeah you're right. Thanks Nev,' I said. 'Take care of yourself, you hear?'

There he was, tied up, bound to the chair, in front of the TV, my sole concession to him, though I didn't switch it on, and I left him to stew in his own shit.

That's how I came by the gun and I must say I was glad it wasn't loaded but, still it was a useful method of intimidating someone. That someone being Rob and also Gloria, who had dropped the handset of the phone.

She's shaking, backing away.

'I don't want any trouble Gloria.' My turn to say those words, with the gun clenched in my hand. Believe me, I really hadn't wanted this to happen. Why can't people be decent? I'd even offered her money. Couldn't she see I was in a fix?

I indicate that she sits, she obliges.

'The money's in my bag, take it, take it all, don't hurt me.'

I don't want her money, I've plenty of my own. Couple of weeks ago, I would have gladly taken it, but now there's no need. What I need is to get out of here and fast.

'Gloria I'm not going to hurt you, no one's going to get hurt.'

'Hands please?'

I'm getting used to this, tying people up. Strange, never in the whole of my life had I the need or desire to do such a thing and now within the space of a week, here I am, for the second time, on my hands and knees with the binding tape, only on this occasion wrapping it round Gloria's thick ankles. 'I'm sorry I have to do this but you can see my predicament.' I bit through the tape and ripped it off the roll.

All tied up with no place to go. That will do nicely. Upending her bag, the contents scattered over the counter, I grab her set of keys.

'See Gloria, I only wanted to borrow your bike. I mean is that such a major deal? And you know what? I'm not going to gag you. You can cry for help the minute I shut this door.'

She isn't saying anything, a stunned expression on her face as I pull the bike helmet off the hook.

Angel is impressed because I haven't resorted to the hard-man act and smashed in Gloria's face just for a laugh like.

I cut the phone wires, take her mobile, switch off the lights, close the door and lock her in. Sorted, there, that wasn't so bad, on cue Gloria begins screaming. Effing this, effing that, I know where you're going, I'll have you picked up . . . Jesus Angel and she did too. I hadn't thought of that. So Angel persuades me to push a hundred quid through the door as some sort of compensation money.

Angel shouts through the keyhole, 'Look we're sorry for the inconvenience Gloria, here's a hundred quid, you'll get your bike back later today. Promise.'

And we hear her sort of burst out laughing.

'Come on Angel.' We scoot round the back of the caff looking for the bike. I'm thinking, motor, moped at the least and round we go again, 'cause the only thing visible is a pushbike. Not even a racer.

'Very funny Gloria.' I pound my fist against the sides of the hut. A hundred quid for this heap of shite. 'Ah man, we could be in big trouble here and for what? I don't trust her. I don't trust this Gloria woman.'

'Let's just get out of here,' says Angel.

No one gets away with making a fool out of me. Those days are long gone.

I go back to the entrance of the caff, unlock the door and switch back on the lights.

'You stupid bitch, why didn't you say you only had a bike. It's hardly worth twenty quid, never mind a hundred. I mean, why make me tie you up, and now Gloria, I really can't be taking any chances, I'm going to have to . . .'

Gloria interrupts me in mid flow. 'I won't say a word.'

'You know I have to meet Fischer, you know he's had an accident. Gloria I'm sorry but the next few hours are important to me, my whole life's riding on it. . . .'

'I swear, I won't say nuffing,' she whimpers pathetically.

'I can't be worrying about it Gloria. You understand don't you? I can't take the risk.' I unwrap her scarf from round her neck. Jesus, I really don't want this to happen, the situation has sort of escalated. I tie the scarf round her eyes then take out the binding tape.

'Please, please,' she's snivelling. The roll of tape is hanging round my fist and I tear off a piece and press it against her mouth.

'Shit Gloria, I'm sorry but I can't take any chances.' Then I pick up the hundred quid, she doesn't deserve it, walk towards the door, flick the lights off and lock her in.

Okay we're ready. 'Angel, are you ready?'

Angel's not answering.

'Are you in a sulk?

'Fuck off.'

What a disaster. I left the thinking to Angel. She's good at that. How has it come to this?

Listen, I only did what I thought was best.

'What if Gloria reports us, hey before you know it she'll have the police on to us and we'll be picked up. We can't take the risk.' Feeling vexed I mount the Triumph Twenty. For Chrissakes, it hasn't even been locked to the railings. Exasperated then to find the bike has only three gears. 'Angel, are you with me?' I snap.

'Shut up Ed and pedal.'

Off we set, Angel sidesaddle and I can tell this isn't going to be an easy ride – one wheel is buckled and the other tyre flat.

Keep the head Ed, keep the head. What a fucking disaster. Shaking the bike in my hands then slamming the damn thing against a wall, I curse that wayward hand of fate.

I had a mind to go back inside and finish the bitch off proper, but we didn't have the time . . . and you know, this was meant to be so easy, Fischer to meet us, drive round to Rob's and now . . .

Could things get any worse?

Stridently pacing down the street, we notice a cab coming straight towards us. Dear God, sweetest of reckonings, to keep the faith and be so rewarded.

I'm humbled by His omnipotence, stand in the middle of the road, my arms waving maniacally.

The cab pulls over, the window's eased down. 'Sorry, I'm off duty.'

Not now, you're not.

'My father, my father's had an accident, he's in hospital, please . . .' Angel to the rescue.

'Look love, I'm on my way home.'

'It's serious . . .' Cue the hysteria, saline droplets of relief and tension cascading down her cheeks.

'Which hospital?'

'Paddington, please . . . please I can pay you.'

'I'll drop you to the nearest police station, that do?'

A resounding negative.

'Please . . . look I've money, a hundred quid, take it, just get me to Paddington.'

He's studying her, those suspicious bruises, and maybe he's thinking she's a runaway from a violent husband.

'Paddington, St Mary's?'

Angel nods her head.

'And you have the money, right? A hundred quid.'

She was waving the two fifties, snatched back from Gloria, and throws them onto the driver's lap.

Already I'm in the back of the cab.

He pushes through a box of tissues.

'Don't worry we'll get you there, soon as possible.'

The car swings round, at last we're on our way.

Isn't it funny how things work out, but isn't it?

'By the way Angel, I thought you were brilliant.'

'Ed, you know your problem? You don't think things through, it's all reaction with you.'

'Instinct and desire, my Angel.'

'What happened back there shouldn't have happened.'

Pushed to extremes and Angel is twitching, her hands shaking so bad, she has to push them into her pockets.

'Calm yourself down love, we'll have you there in no time at all.' The cabbie's voice is reassuring. 'I'm sure he'll be okay.'

You can't be sure of anything these days. There is no such thing as certainty. Angel is livid with me, full of regrets and remorse and imagining Gloria, in the blackness of the caff, waiting to be rescued.

'What a night, eh?'

'The pits,' replies Angel. Her face ashen.

'You're lucky you spotted me.' The cabbie trying his best to calm his passenger down. 'I was just on my way home.'

We were driving through the city and the black cab is warm, warmer than Gloria's, we pass Tower Bridge, hardly any traffic, the streets near empty. I'm reckoning we'll reach the hospital within the next fifteen minutes. An hour's delay at the most, we can still do it. The clock ticking, 4.01 flashes up and I notice the cabbie's identity card, his mugshot. He looks like a good man. An honest man.

On edge again, my head fit to explode, I press the side of my face against the cold of the window.

'Are you all right?'

'No,' Angel interjects. 'Everything's going wrong.'

'I'll just give the wife a bell, let her know what's happening.' He chatters away, I'm half listening.

'She'll be wondering where I've got to.'

'What?' says Angel.

'The wife, she'll be worried . . .' Out with his mobile and he dials a number.

There I am looking at his mugshot thinking is he? isn't he? and this is exactly what occurs to me as Gloria's mobile starts ringing in my pocket.

How about that for synchronicity?

STOP. This situation had gone beyond the beyond, it had gotten out of hand, hands in the pockets of my jacket trying to find Gloria's blasted phone. I should have tossed it aside, but I hadn't and neither had Angel. She lets out a small whimper. This doesn't bode well. Don't take out the gun. *Not yet.* I pull out Gloria's mobile, switch it off and pretend to have a conversation. Look, I was trying my hardest to contain the predicament we were now enmeshed in.

'How is he? is he going to make it . . .' Attempting to sound realistic, yet at the same time not draw attention to myself.

Sniffle sniffle, knees knocking, I slunk back down in the seat.

In the rear-view mirror the driver was staring straight at me. Actually he was boring a hole straight through my forehead.

'They've taken him down to theatre,' I gasped, this ludicrous one-way conversation with myself, totally unconvincing. Gloria's husband wasn't interested in my prittle-prattle.

'Let's pray he makes it.' I shoved the phone back in my bag, felt nauseous, something was going to give.

Angels lips purse tight. She's sweating. Christ, how I wish she wasn't so conspicuous.

The cabbie swings a sharp right. Act dumb, you know nothing.

La la la when I find myself la la la trouble . . .

He swings another right. Semi-circle.

We're off course, in deep shit and the driver is dialling Gloria for a second time.

'Dead,' he mutters.

Like Sal, just like Sal.

I surmise he must have called the caff phone. 'Jesus Christ . . .' and he's done a little arithmetic, put two and two together. Mr Cabbie must have been on his way to collect her when we appeared. Gloria's espresso phone-call would have been to him, she likely made some remark or other about us, along the lines of . . . weirdos . . . we're going to have do something and fast.

'What have you done to her?' he shouts through to us.

The meatballs rise in my throat, pressing down the handle, open you bitch . . .

Holy shit here we go again . . . Tumbling out and run rabbit run.

Scramble to my feet, can hear the screech of his tyres into

reverse, as he gives good backward chase. Sprinting fast as possible, Angel right with me, thank God for one-way systems, down a no-entry street we flee. He's out of the cab and running, a knuckle-duster misses me by millimetres. Don't look behind, he won't catch up, not with his huge bulbous beer-belly. Can hear the sound of a slamming door.

'We've made it Angel,' my chest heaving. 'Angel we've made it.'

Hands on my knees, panting. Catch my breath. We begin walking southward and hit the Thames.

'You dildo,' sneers Angel.

'Yeah thanks, like I really need your support.'

'How much further do you think we'll get before the police pick us up?'

'We'll get there Angel.'

'You think nice Mr Cabbie is going to just drive off and leave it at that?'

'And what would you have done?'

'Well I wouldn't have tied up Gloria in the first place.'

'Fuck Gloria,' and I toss her mobile over the wall into the water.

Tate Britain on the right, not too far from Victoria station, we can hail another cab.

'Ed, every black cab in this city will have been alerted by now.'

She's right of course, we'll have to catch a night bus.

'Ed we are in so deep.'

'Sure babe but we're not drowning.'

Thinking once more of what had already happened to Sal, Frank, Neville, sure the business with Gloria and her husband is but a minor blunder in comparison. Shit, I mean look how far we've already come.

Angel's anger subsides. Breathing regular again and there's colour in her cheeks.

It was only a few days ago when we met, seems like an eternity. My silent partner, lost in our own thoughts we're walking up Vauxhall Bridge Rd towards Victoria station.

There isn't much point going to the hospital now, not to be welcomed by PC Plod, the authorities would have been alerted, no doubt about it. We'll have to find an alternative meeting place. Somewhere safe, indoors, not Neville's, for all I know Nev could still be stewing. Fischer's place is way off the mark. Fischer, we'll have to call him and let him know what's happened.

Angel dials his mobile number but it switches straight to answerphone.

'Fischer, where the hell are you? We're heading towards Paddington, listen there's been some complications so we're going to have to meet up someplace else. Call when you get this message.'

A safe place, think Goddamit . . . think . . .

Blank blank, blankety-blank, low on cash I'd stolen her chequebook and pen, little girl laugh and she'd smelt quite fishy . . .

Imelda. Dear sweet Imelda of Shirland Road. Now there's a twinkling possibility.

'Who the fuck's Imelda?' pipes up Angel.

'Ahh just this girl I met, no one special.'

'You never mentioned her before.'

'Why, should I have?'

'Well . . . yeah Ed, the way you go on about Sal and how much you loved her and how she betrayed you and how everything you do is in her memory . . .'

'You jealous Angel?'

'Get real.'

The long and the short of it amounted to a few nights of white girl flesh, Irish and perverted. Mmm smacking my lips together, with Sal gone and she'd been gone a good twenty-four hours, well what's a man to do.

Succumb, easily.

I had desires, needs, wants. I'd had an almighty flush of energy after Sal had pegged it. Perhaps it was the smell of lingering death I'd hoped to erase, a sense of her still clung, or maybe it was the fact all of her stuff was in Neville's and a constant reminder or the thrill of the act that had got me going. The why of it is not actually of consequence. What happened was, I woke up on Sal's settee, up in Neville's flat, and it was just past midnight and I had an overwhelming urge to get laid.

Neville was snoring loudly. I left him to it and headed down to Camden. Thursday night, wide awake, wondering where on earth would be a good place to pick up an easy fuck. Waited fifteen minutes for a tube, most people on the homeward bound, most of them smelling of drink. Bum Central, stark light, plenty of empty seats and the unwanted innards of papers fluttering haplessly. I got a seat, hopped off at Leicester Square, crossed over through Chinatown and then to Soho. The whole area was buzzing, blasts of fresh aftershave, assaulting my nostrils, groups of guys, shrill and dramatic in their gestures.

We, Sal and I, hadn't done anything like this for such a long while, no minor social explosions of great entertainment value. The majority of our evenings had been spent inside, catching up on videos. Blockbuster nights, bringing the cinema home to you; bit of an exaggeration, not even on a DVD flat-screened mega TV. It's not that an evening in can't be nice, snuggled up on the sofa with a bottle of wine and take-away pizza, but when it becomes the social high-light of your week you're heading for trouble, may as well be camped out in suburbia with a couple of kids. Her excuse banal and annoying, 'But Ed I don't feel like going out, I can't be bothered, I'm tired' . . . and of course we always had to watch these crap emotional fanny films about relation-ships and love.

Unleashed from Sal's noose there came a desert thirst needing to be quenched and high on a feeling of elation and rekindled freedom, I was sweet of tooth and sought out the Candy Bar; the place was basically dripping in pussy. Mmmmm yummy.

In I went.

Should have made more of an effort, there were a lot of very hot women. Many pierced, great worked-out bodies, hardcore lesbo chic, I like a challenge, and then there was Imelda.

She'd been stood up, it was sadly blatant, sat on a stool at the bar with a sad expression on her face. She had this air of a person who tried too hard, like she wanted to be fucked over. The best thing about Imelda was her hair, long, black, shiny curls.

Fair damsel in distress may I? I outward pondered and she gave me the green light.

'A bloody Mary.'

'Make that two, butch tender.' I handed over a tenner and squeezed in closer beside Imelda. 'My dear you look like you've lost a pound and found a penny.'

I complimented her on her physique and beauty, opened my ears so she could spill all those minor anxieties in. Young, she had recently turned twenty-one, a student of the arts and media and was on the cusp of coming out. This was supposed to be *the* night but the woman she had meant to be meeting had failed to show. 'Maybe,' Imelda pondered, 'maybe it's an omen,' and she wasn't really cut out for it. I told her the night was just beginning. Her belly was pierced but a reaction had caused much oozing and there was a plaster slapped on her pale skin. She was slightly plump with a huge pair of breasts and her makeup shovelled on. She'd do for the night and I poured as much alcohol down our respective throats as I could manage. We ended up back in her flat. She shared it with a couple of Australians and an out-of-work actor. It was damp and she was all giggly, slightly embarrassed, stumbling around, offering me toast and instant coffee.

'Come here.' I issued the order gently and she complied, cigarette breath, and I ran my fingers through her hair. If Sal could see me now, she'd have been disgusted, her stomach would have churned. I think I wanted it that way, to do stuff that would have appalled her.

We moved into Imelda's bedroom. I sat on her futon watching her strip, her performance clumsy and badly orchestrated, like she was thinking of what to do next, the next step.

'What do you want me to do?' she asked. 'How is it you want me?'

I was more aroused by the situation than the events, Imelda trying her hardest to be sexy or her interpretation of what sexy was. She flopped down naked on the bed beside me and I, cupping her soft breasts, then exercised my tongue.

'You can do what ever you want.' Her voice was soft and lyrical.

'Well now let me see . . .' and I did my best to put her at ease, our first outing slightly messy and self-conscious.

'Stay the night,' she whispered, gripping me tight around the waist, curling her body up into mine.

'Mmm,' already half asleep. A little porn star at my side, wanting to play the good catholic, with her dirty mind and guilty conscience.

She woke me up next morning with breakfast in bed, toast and marmalade. She mentioned the fact she thought we'd make a good a couple. I took a shower, felt a bit tacky. On my way out, she stopped me,

'Aren't you forgetting something?'

'Ehh . . .' She reminded me of absent manners. 'My number,' and giggling she pressed a piece of paper into my hand.

'Oh yeah.' I'd forgotten there were certain courtesies to be paid. I took my leave saying I'd call her.

When? Whenever.

I could tell Imelda wanted a bastard, I could do that.

Walking up though Maida Vale to Little Venice I hit the canal and walked straight through to Camden.

'Ed?' perks up Angel nudging an elbow into my side. 'Did you think Imelda was cheap?'

'And nasty.'

Know what? I wanted to feel what Rob felt towards Sal, put myself in his shoes. It was an experiment, see how easy it was to abuse someone from a position of dominance.

'Did you see her again?'

'Sure, when I was feeling aggressive or wanting to assert myself. The harder I was on Imelda the more she begged for it. The more she clung. You'll see. She thinks she's fallen in love with me.'

Our rhythmic strides had taken us to the top of the wide road. The mobile begins bleeping, it's Fischer.

'Fischer!!'

Clink, clink, he's ringing from a payphone.

'Listen we got into a bit of trouble back there.'

'I know . . . your blue friends waiting, I have been questioned already.'

So he knows and I'm beginning to understand.

'Meet us at Imelda's, you remember . . . I told you about the weird chick on Shirland Road.'

'I say I do not know you but they hope you show.'

'Just get your ass over to Imelda's as soon as you can . . .' and cut out the middle men, 'huh?'

'My leg in cast. Impossible.'

Is he purposely trying to screw things for us?

'I thought you said it was your neck.'

'Fracture to lower tibia.'

Tibia, fibia . . . 'So . . .'

'They keep me overnight observation.'

'It's morning already.'

'What?'

'You saying I have to come and get you?'

'Ward 3B, third floor.'

'Shit.'

We turn the corner outside Victoria Station, stop by a soft drinks machine, throw back a couple more paracetamols, then join the tail-end of a long queue, ready to board a wait-ing bus. We shuffle forward. Good God but I will never understand why they got rid of conductors. It doesn't make the slightest bit of sense. I give the driver a quid and tear off the slip of a ticket. Climbed the stairs hoping to find a free seat but to no avail, no spaces on the top deck and back down we go, edging our way towards the rear. A kindly gent offers up his seat for Angel. What a nice gesture, after every-thing that has happened, it's good to see there are still people in this world who care, manners do exist though sometimes you have to dig hard.

Of course, the fact that the gent has been sitting next to a minging bum may have something to do with his generosity. Angel slides down in the seat and she fits in all too well, her side comrade being in a similar state, they could be a couple.

My present psyche. Weighing up the pros and cons from a position of zero. Much like when I'd done away with Sal. An initial feeling of invincibility that we would make it, some-how or other.

Fischer could wallow in the comfort of an NHS bed a little longer. I was calm, intensely focused on the present. There was nothing to lose by going for it, a lesson learnt some six weeks ago, for there was absolutely no alternative. Teetering on the edge renders panic and doubt useless emotions. A loss of self-confidence can be fatal.

Besides, I was pretty certain Frank would have, by now, employed some authority or other to get me, having unloaded all that money from him. I really didn't under-stand why he got so upset over a trifling twelve grand, having practically offered it to me in the first place.

Bags of cash to get rid of Sal. I had relieved him of his

money to ease his troubled conscience, to make Sal disappear for good. Quite a feat, seeing as she was already out of the way.

The morning I waved ta-da to Imelda, thanking her for her warm and generous hospitality, off I set through Little Venice. A charming spot of wealth and tweedom, of houseboats hung with flowers and ornaments, ornate bridges boardered by Georgian houses with creamy fronts and gardens, creating an impression of seclusion from the dirt and stress of the metropolis. I walked along the canal towpath, full of what had transpired the night before. That which I had accomplished, for I had felt the victory of Imelda's tremors three times, not bad eh? Okay this is not so much a boast as a revelation. She was butter in my hands, soft and unctuous. Three times the coming and I congratulated myself as I passed over Edgware Road to rejoin the canal at the bottom of Aberdeen Place.

The most gloomy part of the canal, surrounded by mushrooming council estates, ugly and in stark contrast to the scenic beauty on offer across the road. That's London, without boundaries, a mix of hotch-potch extremes, cultures and infested by too many people living in too close a proximity.

I wished Sal could have witnessed my prowess with Imelda. How I would have gloated, for she had always mocked my impotency. There, I've said it, I could never satisfy Sal. She said I always left her aching, I couldn't reach her the way other men did. It was not for the want of trying. I'd labour hard but she would curl her legs up and turn her back to me. This is not good, she'd say, not right, this isn't how it's meant to be – Is there ever a right way? And she turned from me at every opportunity, provoking in me a terrible insecurity. Less than zero. Then to be slapped in the face with her infidelities and the fact she could so effortlessly succumb to another, without a thought for me.

When she finished with Rob, like for the final, final time, for the relationship had buoyed in an unhealthy manner, I assumed, I was, at last, in with a chance. I was, but not wholly, never totally. I would always suffer the stigma of being second best, for at every given chance she would veer away from me and squander herself on Rob. He was an opportunist to the end. In fact he was the one killing her, surely he held responsibility because he had triggered her decline. If he had cared for Sal one iota, things might have been different. Even during their relationship he fucked around, as if there was a death sentence hanging over his dick. His entire sense of masculinity wrapped tight within his foreskin. So zealous was he in his conquests, Sal became crippled by blindness. I watched as he poisoned her into a state of gradual debilitation, where conqueror and vanquished cohabited in mutual moral decline. He would have had to hate her, as I came to hate her, we had that much in common. As he undid Sal, I swore I would undo him. Sal thought I was useless, how wrong of her, three times Imelda, dirty girl. If only Sal had given me a proper chance but alas, it was too late.

Such were my deliberations as I walked along the side of Regents Park, past the zoo, beneath the aviary, enjoying early stirrings of a freedom I had thought unattainable. You know the first thing I was wanting to do?

Write a host of letters, scrawl out a million putrefying words to every person who'd ever fucked me over.

Dear Mrs Simpson,

I heard about your third miscarriage, I can't tell you how good that made me feel. You sad shitbag of scum. Even your body revolts against you. Ha you bully bitch. Oh don't you remember, Class 2a and your little humiliation ritual. If it wasn't for you I would have been Class Captain (at that age these things mattered a great deal). Long may you remain barren . . .

Dear Dr Fuckface Gordon,

So your filth-fingers have finally curled up in arthritic pain. You dry old goat, I've always wondered about your treatment of me. Very unorthodox in retrospect, tut-tut, a big disappointment you were, considering your stature and position . . .

Puerile vilifications in the extreme, but amusing none the less and I mounted the steps up by the Anglican church on the edge of Primrose Hill and headed down towards Parkway. My head was clearing as the realization took hold that I could do whatever it was I fancied, food for thought, and I opened the door to George's and ordered a full fat fry-up. No more half measures or living in a self-imposed state of enslavement. That I had taken a life was one thing but I would argue it was self-defence, indeed in defence of my very being. I had to do it, I was so wrapped up in her.

A fistful of fork punctured the egg yolk and I watched as it seeped over the beans and muddy mushrooms. What now, to lord it, give in to every temptation. I aimed to live royally and sup with kings.

The waitress handed me the bill. I had been there two hours, clinging on to the plate and dregs of coffee, twice replenished. What now? and I took out Imelda's chequebook and let her pay for my lunch. Hey, I'd spent a fortune on her the night before. Resources had already dwindled, cash deficit. I left the restaurant under scrutiny. Went to the market to cash a few of Imelda's cheques at various disreputable stalls and managed to exact a measly two hundred quid. It would have to do but was hardly enough to transport me anywhere exotic. Money was uppermost in my mind and, listing everything I wanted, I had spent double that by the time I got to the traffic lights on my way back to Neville's flat.

As for my own fiscal resources, I had none. Broke, I had been living off of Sal for a good while, a fact I'd come to loathe, being morally traditional and regarded it as a weakness in her, that she should have allowed me to leech off her for so long. Poverty is not a happy state, it straitjackets you and at the very least is frustrating and tiresome. Sal was the careful sort, she joined store schemes in the hope of accumulating x amount of points, so she could get a discounted ferry ride to Dieppe with a five-pound voucher to splash out on a bottle of plonk, providing she'd already bought ten quid's worth of the nasty vinegar. No, this was not my idea of freedom. Money buys freedom and access to all areas. My desire was to be handed a large wad of cash. A huge free gift, the likelihood of which was bleak.

Back to the flats I strode and when I reached the block, I caught a glimpse of Frank, as he swung out of the building and scooted over to his racy Peugeot.

Now there was someone I could bleed dry.

The Ultimate Money Shot

Hey Frankieeeeee, don't you remember, me! A Sister Sledge
number, Sal had lost her virginity to, way, way, back in the
mists of time, during a friend's twenty-first at the far side of
a marquee, directly behind where the band played and where
two other cherries were popped that very same night.

Frank drove too fast, his tyres screeched and off sped one
very wealthy man.

On the ascent to Neville's flat I stopped by our old abode.
Pinned to the door was a note marked 'Sal'. I ripped it off,
unfolded it and read.

Sal,

Where are you? We are all really worried, I know
things have been tough on you this last while, so if
there is anything I can do and I mean <u>anything</u> . . .
just give me a call.

By the way we got the commission through, good
news!

lots of love, Frank

Lots of love, offering anything . . . and in the circumstances an offer I'd find hard to refuse.

'Tickets please.' An inspector boards the bus, his accusatory mantra hoping to catch one of us out, we are all of us guilty and must prove our innocence, the 'modern' way.

'Tickets please?' hoping to enlighten a passenger of ten pounds or else.

'Tickets please,' as he wades up the galley, clipping holes in scraps of paper with ads on the back. Can't see nothing out the windows and I wonder where we are, how far we've gotten. Angel must have drowsed off again 'cause her head rests upon the tramp's shoulder. I watch disgusted as the tramp pulls the ticket still clutched in her hands and makes out it's his. The inspector chooses to ignore Angel and lets her sleep, perhaps he glimpses her floating halo; however he turns sharpish to me.

'Tickets please.' My own, torn into tiny pieces, has met with the same fate as the wedding invitation. It's a bad habit, nothing serious, but the inspector won't accept its metamorphosis. Bastard.

I refuse to give him a tenner. I've already spent a hundred quid and look how far that has got us. Adamant, I kick up a verbal fuss and alight from the vehicle with Angel in tow.

Boy, are we relieved to find we've only gone one stop further than where we should have got off. Inadvertently a favour has been done.

To Imelda's we trudge, faster, faster, time slipping forward at an incredible rate. The rain spits at intervals, its spirit broken, coughing up the last of its load.

·

'Must be half four by now or more.' Angel quiet beside me, her feet sodden through and when we reach the front door, the first thing she wonders is if it would be okay to ask Imelda for a loan of a pair of socks.

'Angel, we're going the whole hog here.'

'What d'you mean?'

The plan being to get to Fischer undetected. From our previous conversation there's a high probability that the police are waiting at St Mary's; an Angel in disguise is the only way in.

See no point in waking up the entire household so I rap on Imelda's bedroom window.

I hadn't seen Imelda for a few weeks, guessed she'd be mad at me, being under the impression there was something going on between us. I'd done my best to convey the opposite but she wasn't convinced. The last time we met, I'd let her take me out for dinner and she'd given me a present of a Claddagh ring. A love token indicating one's status. I put it on the wrong way round. She was in a bit of a state, freaked out, saying how she suspected someone in the house was robbing her. Besides her chequebook, I'd also managed to nab a bit of her jewellery to pawn, this pre Frank's generous bequeathment.

Missy Imelda where art thou? For there comes no reply to my knocking. How sad that she should miss out on such a romantic gesture.

'She's out Ed.'

Silly trollop and I call her on the mobile, her answer service kicking in straight off. Dialled once more to see if I can hear a response coming from the room. Nothing and I was glad of it. Hadn't particularly wanted to see her in the first place, most probably she would have told me to fuck off. I try easing her window open, it budges all of an inch before hitting off a lock.

'Let's hope one of the Aussies is home.'

Finger on the buzzer. Angel squelching her feet in her trainers, uninterested in my impatience.

'I mean can you believe this? Come on . . . someone answer the door . . .'

We waited about five minutes before an upstairs window rattled open and a head appeared.

'God it's five in the morning.'

'Hi there, I'm a friend of Imelda's.'

'What do you want?'

'Can I come in?'

'Imelda isn't here.'

'I know, look I need help, will you let us in. Please?'

'No offence but I don't know you.'

I could see his hands were ready to push the window down.

'Wait, you're the out of . . . I mean the actor right? Imelda's told me all about you. You're Tim, right? I know this is weird but . . . I need your help. Please let us in, I can explain everything.'

Imelda had told me Tim was up his own arse big time. I'd have to appeal to his vanity.

He slams down the window.

'Thank God for that Angel and remember to smile.' I squeeze her hand, cold and clammy. Damp through and through.

We listen to the encroaching steps, as he shuffles towards the door, unlocks it and a very pissed-off Tim ushers us inside.

'Look I'm really sorry to disturb you and thanks . . .'

He has turned on the hall lamp and is shocked by the state of Angel's face.

'What happened . . . were you attacked?'

'Yeah,' and Angel presses her palm over her mouth as if to suppress a glut of sobs. 'I'm in trouble, there's this guy . . . I didn't know where to go, Imelda was my last resort.'

We play the compassion card, the helpless victim. Have a heart. Angel spun a big lie, she explained how it began a few weeks ago when she'd met this geezer through a classified ad. 'I'm not a freak . . . I just wanted to experience something different . . .'

'Sure, I can relate,' Tim answers. 'Acting's all about that, subjecting yourself to different scenarios.'

'Yeah but it all got out of hand,' Angel continues on her tangent, telling Tim how this psycho guy had become obsessed and started stalking her. A few days ago he'd set upon her and beaten her up, hence her face.

'Why didn't you call the police?'

'I did,' and Tim's jaw drops a further inch as she relates the story of how she called the police and he'd been sent round. 'He told me he was going to kill me.'

'Fuck sakes.' Tim's eyes are near popping from his skull.

'I've been so weirded out and then tonight, I was lying in bed and I'm in a basement flat and I can hear someone rattling at the door.'

'What did you do?'

'I ran for it, that's why I'm here.'

'Man, that is so wild.'

Isn't it just and Tim swallows it whole.

'I need to lay low for a while.'

'Sure well . . . stay here for the night.'

'Nah I can't take the risk, he may be following.'

'Oh my God!'

Time to intervene before Angel goes way off the scales of reality. 'Imelda told me, she said you're really talented.'

'Yeah, shit do you think he'll break in here. Should I call the police?'

'No don't do anything yet. So . . . so where is she?' I ask. 'Imelda?'

'Her and the Aussies have gone to Amsterdam for the weekend. Look are you okay?'

Do we look okay? I don't think so, bedraggled and bruised.

'The thing is . . . I was hoping Imelda could spare some clothes.'

'I see . . .'

'I really appreciate this Tim . . . I can't tell you . . .'

'Don't worry, it's okay.'

Imelda had makeup and lots of it, Imelda had clothes and lots of them and Imelda also had a wig. Oh, didn't I mention it?

At the Candy Bar, the thing that had attracted me to Imelda was her hair, lush, shiny, long and black. Back at hers later that night, unexpectedly, her scalp had shifted in my hand.

'A wig!' Surprised I was and slightly disconcerted.

She'd grinned at me, like a kid who'd been found out. 'Me own hair was so mankey . . . Arlene was in the shower and I was in a rush. Are you disappointed, I mean lots of women wear wigs. Are you okay?'

Short changed I felt fooled, the hair thing had worked. Tricking me into thinking she was acceptable in physical terms. She'd cheated me, her eyes were blue and I liked the blue/black combination, found out later her true colour was a mousy hue and her eyes grey. It truly was offputting to discover I'd pulled a dog.

We follow Tim down the hall corridor to Imelda's room, my fingers crossed that she hadn't taken the wig away with her. Her stuff littered all over the place. Tim appears totally intrigued by Angel.

He put his arm round her. 'This is so heavy, listen if there's anything I can do?'

'I need to get to Paddington, take the express and just get out of here for a while.'

'Yeah sure, listen don't worry . . .'

Angel's just the best and as if on cue we hear footsteps pass outside.

Shocked into silence and then Tim whispers that he'll do her up. Apparently he studied makeup technique as part of his acting course.

'Would you? Tim, thanks, thanks so much.'

He runs upstairs to his room to get his palate and brushes.

'Angel, I love you.' Hand on my heart. 'Do you think he's gay?'

She smiles. 'Who cares,' pulling off her clothes. I've been scrummaging through all of Imelda's stuff, picked out a short skirt and high boots, for the sexy, secretary look. Came across the wig lying discarded at the bottom of Imelda's wardrobe.

Tim calls out from behind the door, 'Can I come in?'

Zipping up the skirt and pulling over a tight sweater I give Angel the once over, already she looks halfway decent and in Tim comes.

'What do you think?'

'Way too cheap, especially as you're going to wear the hair.'

Perhaps he's a fag, though he has a point and we go up to the Aussie girl's room and check out her wardrobe. Much more street cred, better labels too and there's the dress, the one Sal had seen in Selfridges, the day she'd had her bag nicked. Angel tries it on and it fits just right.

'Do you think she'll mind me borrowing her clothes?'

'I wouldn't worry about it. Arlene is loaded.' Tim doesn't like Arlene, her London experience is padded and propped by her father, a huge-shot businessman, so we're categorically not to feel guilty.

Guilt, well that's just an emotion which fails to orbit my world.

Guilt was much more Sal's thing. And she would beat herself up for feeling this and thinking that, for not having been nicer to her kid brother, for not stopping to escort the blind lady as she crossed the road, for mistakenly barging to the top of a two-person queue, for war victims, animals, refugees, white trash, black trash. She made a point of not being racist. For leading Frank on.

It was my fault, all of it. I should have known we'd end up sleeping together, if only I hadn't worn that short skirt. I'd come to memorize most of Sal's diary, the important bits anyhow. The bits that propelled me to take action. *Frank is decent it's just . . . it would never work.* Did she honestly think he actually wanted her? All he wanted was a dip, a honeypot plunge and fast fuck. How Sal could even think Frank would feel guilty over his actions was beyond me. *I feel I may have hurt him.* The man had no feelings. He was slime.

When I took Frank up on his kindly offer of help this is what he said: 'That stupid fucking bitch. And you tell her from me, if I ever see her again, she's dead.' These were his exact words as he handed over the money.

Sat at the end of the Aussie's bed, Tim sets about transforming my Angel so that all bruises vanish beneath foundation and cover-up. My hands tightly clasped on the backpack, as Angel flirts with Tim.

'You've very striking features,' she says to him. 'I bet you look great on camera.'

'Actually a lot of people have said that.'

I leave them to it.

Wanna know something? All those hate letters I was meant to write, well I never got round to writing any of them; all my energy went into blackmailing Frank.

Dear Frank,

This is really difficult for me to put into words, so I may as well tell you straight, I'm pregnant. I went to the doctors a few days ago, basically that's why I haven't been at work. The night we made love [*it physically hurt me to write those two words*], I conceived, even though I had taken the morning-after pill. No doubt this will come as a great shock and God alone knows what your reaction will be but believe me Frank, it's definitely yours. The thing is, it's too late to do anything about it and I'm going to have to keep the baby. I never wanted this to happen and have spent the last few days thinking, about us and the baby and what I should do. The day you called by the flat I'd been walking down by the canal trying to straighten out my head. I must have just missed you but when I read the note you left, I knew that no matter how hard it is going to be for you to digest this, you are a true friend and do care about me. I know you'll never leave your wife and I wouldn't want you to, so please do believe me when I say I don't want to make trouble for you. In fact I think it would be best for all concerned if I move away. I'm considering going to Brighton and bringing up the baby there. I really hope we wont fall out over this and will remain close friends. We need to talk, I'm staying at the above address and you can contact me on the mobile. For all our sakes (yours, your family, our baby and I), please call when you get this letter.

Lots of love,
Sal.

I hand delivered it, strode right into the offices and left it at reception. Weasley Frank must have tossed the letter in the bin, because no reply came and after three days I stepped up the campaign. I had suspected Frank was fairly gutless and obviously shit scared. He'd deny everything hoping it would go away.

Another letter was duly dispatched.

Dear Frank,

I know you're not out of the country. I was down by the offices yesterday and saw you. I'm sure you must be very shocked 'cause I haven't heard from you but your silence is terrifyingly ominous for me. Please don't turn your back on the situation. Call me as soon as you get this.

   Love,

   Sal

Again I delivered it by hand. Again no forthcoming reply. In vain I scribbled another.

Dear Frank,

   I'm trying to keep calm but please, please I beg you Frank do get in touch, we need to talk.

   Heartfelt wishes,

   Sal.

On behalf of Sal, I began to call Frank at the office but he was always busy. More letters, more calls, all met by a stony resilient silence.

   This was during my piss-poor period in the first two weeks after Sal's demise. Frank's flat refusal to communicate irked me somewhat; imagine if Sal really had been pregnant, what a bastard. I put myself in her shoes,

Frank,

   I don't understand why you are doing this to me. Please can't we at least talk about it. Please Frank, I'll call by the office tomorrow or if you'd rather, call me today at 3 p.m.

   Yours lovingly,

   Sal.

*

Down I trotted to the office, handed in the letter, waited for a response, three o'clock chimed and *bleep, bleep* . . .

   'You fucking bitch.'

'It's Ed actually.'

'Put me on to Sally.'

'She's really upset, you've really upset her Frank. The doctor has her under sedation and by the way she's got a sick note, so you won't be able to dismiss her unfairly.'

'Are you trying to threaten me?'

'I don't think I have to. As a loving father, you already know the cost of child maintenance.'

'So what are you trying to say?'

'It's pretty obvious to Sal you don't want anything to do with her, shame that, but there you go, happens all the time. See the thing is . . .'

'Get on with it.'

'See Frank, the thing is Sal's smashed broke, if she goes away now, primarily to protect you and your family she'll settle for a lump sum, loss of earnings and the maternity benefit she'd be due.'

'I don't have listen to this crap. As far as I'm concerned I'm not the father.'

'Oh but you are.'

'Prove it.'

How wonderful the advances in medical science but I didn't have nine months to play with. I needed the money straightaway. Sal would have given him the benefit of the doubt. At least she'd have listed out her projected loss of earnings and any benefits due. Prospective budgeting was her forte and she was always great with other people's money, though hopeless with her own. I sent Frank a proposal, including all the figures at hand, added on a bit here, a bit there, but it amounted to the tidy sum of £30,000.

'You are out of your mind. You're a friggin' fruitcake.' The response was disheartening to say the least. I had to threaten Frank, outlined how detrimental it would be for him and his family should it come to light . . . Man, but he wasn't budging. It was nearly three weeks since my campaign began. Freedom was somewhat curtailed without adequate finances. Petty thievery wasn't my deal, besides I didn't want to get nicked over something banal, when Sal's life, or 'lack of', was hanging round my neck.

Since Sal's death, I'd been staying one floor up at Neville's. No one seemed to noticed her absence, bar Frank, the reality was no one was even looking for her. I had managed to sell or pawn all of Sal's detritus, everything I'd originally given to Nev. He was real peeved about it, saying it wasn't right to give with the one hand and take with the other.

'What you on about Nev? I never gave you nothing, it was all on loan, a mere loan.' I played dumb and pleaded ignorance.

He started saying how I was taking advantage of him.

'Neville get real. You're the type who will always be taken advantage of.'

Neville told me he didn't want me staying with him any more.

'That's not very nice Nev, I thought we were friends.'

He was glued to the TV, scowling 'cause I kept confusing him.

'Look Nev, don't worry about it, it will all work out in the end. Holy shit.' Staring through the window my gaze focused on a Hiace Van and followed it into the yard. I watched as it pulled up outside the block.

'Shit Nev . . .'

'What Ed?'

Roly-poly Coleen emerged from the passenger side of the van, then Kevin and Roger from the driver's side.

'What you on about Ed?'

'Coleen's here.' The long-awaited arrival, the flat vacant for three weeks. I hadn't forgotten, just put it to the back of my mind.

'You're right Neville, it's time I left you in peace.'

'Ed, it's just that you're really mean to me.'

'I know but it's so easy, I can't help it.'

'Where are you going?'

'Dunno, do you have any money?' I asked, knowing full well he'd just cashed his benefits cheque.

He wasn't completely stupid and had the gall to reply in the negative.

'Hey Ed!' he barked as I'd switched off the TV, 'What the . . . man you are such a . . .'

'Hush, I gotta hear what happens.'

I crouched down by the floor, Sal's old flat directly below us. Neville knelt beside me, snap clicking his fingers,

'Man they are going to be soooo pissed at what you did to their flat.'

Yep they most certainly were.

Clear as crystal, like they could have been in the same room.

'That bitch, that bitch is –' they were, of course, referring to Sal 'is dead.'

Yep, she most certainly was.

Left in no uncertain terms about their attitude to Sal, I waited up in Neville's till I was sure they'd gone, managed to wangle all of Neville's weekly benefit and fled.

*

'Okay you can open your eyes now,' Tim announces, proud of his work.

My, my . . . but would you look at Angel.

I quite like this Tim, an all-round decent chap, subtle in his artistry, colouring Angel's face so that she looks normal not vampish.

We put a hairnet over her scalp and attach the wig.

Hey presto and, 'Know what Angel, you're one hell of a good-looking lady.'

'Why thank you Ed.'

'Tim, you've done an amazing job, very talented.'

'Well, I've had a nice face to work on.'

Aw shucks and it's time to go.

'Thanks Tim, and I promise to send back the clothes and wig and . . .'

'How are you getting to Paddington? I'll give you lift if you want.'

A car . . . the guy has a car. God sent Tim and we were ready and waiting. Maybe now is the time to offer him money.

Angel pinches me hard.

'I'm not going through that again, Ed.'

Anyhow Tim doesn't have a car, he has a Domino's Pizza bike.

'Keeps me in money till I hit the big time.'

'Makes a lot of sense Tim. Yeah, don't give up the day job.'

'D'you have everything?' he asks Angel.

'Money, passport, tickets, gun.'

'Are you serious? You have a gun?' Tim reckons Angel could be a New Avenger and I really am beginning to respect this guy, he's very perceptive. An avenger. That's exactly what Angel is.

'Well a girl's got to take care of herself. It's not a real one mind.'

We leave the house, an approaching dawn beckons casting shadows through the darkness. The skies are clear, it looks like it may be a nice day.

A nice day, for a white wedding.

Sal had always wanted a traditional do, had imagined the scenario a zillion times, she'd even bought bridal magazines and gone to boutiques to try on dresses.

Swirling and twirling in front of me, she'd wistfully enquire, 'What do you think?'

'I think you are deceiving yourself, white isn't a colour you can wear.'

'What about off-white?'

'What about a shroud?'

There she'd be gushing at extravagantly hideous dresses, chatting with the assistants about her forthcoming imaginary wedding to Rob.

Poor Sal and it's moments like these when I think of her naivety and it makes me want to puke.

'You okay back there?' shouts Tim.

'Sure are.' Key in the ignition and vroom . . . vroom . . .

Paddington here we come.

Angel is squashed up close against Tim, false black hair blowing in the wind and bare knees encapsulating Tim's thighs. It's a tight fit and she leans in close so that her whole torso presses up next to his back and her face turns to the side, her nose level with his neck. Intimately entangled and I can't resist the temptation.

'Angel maybe you could leave a lasting impression?'

'I already am.'

'You know what I mean.'

'What, show Tim how appreciative we are of his efforts?'

Her hands are wrapped around his waist and I'm thinking it would be a nice gesture if they lowered a little and perhaps even slid down inside his jeans.

'And jerk him off?'

It's an idea, a little dirty, but I like it, imagine Tim would be in his element, he could dine out on the story for years to come.

'And what would I get Ed?'

'Sticky fingers.'

Why is it, I wonder, we find it so difficult to give without receiving anything ourselves. To give freely, without any expectation of a favour in return.

No, this is the truth, I'm thinking of Rob and his sleazeball antics.

'Let's regard it as a last fling, like a pre-Rob warm-up, a practice run. You know what I'm getting at Angel?'

We've been through this over and over. What will happen, when we arrive up at Rob's. It has all been planned out.

'I'll do it for Sal,' Angel smirks.

This should have been Sal's night. In a manner of speaking, Sal's hen night, though she'd have expected nothing more than a drunken evening with the girls in a cheapo restaurant with a stripper thrown in for good measure and a dildo to wave about. She'd have thought that risqué, such a laugh, 'a ha ha ha'.

'Angel, think of the pleasure you'll be imparting.'

Angel hums and haws but I know she's up for it. The idea hasn't repulsed her and she pushes her crotch further against

Tim's butt. She likes Tim, he's sweet and it's obvious he likes her. Who wouldn't like my Angel? You only have to look at her to know she's pure, bruises and all. She's an honest soul.

'Hey Angel, regard it as something you could write home about.'

She flinches. 'If, Ed, I had a home.'

'It'll happen. Don't be so impatient.'

Angel had been sleeping on floors and sofas for so long now, she couldn't recall the anchoring feeling of pushing a key in the door to disappear inside and leave the world behind. A quiet, private space where you could close your eyes and not worry in case someone was watching. I'd tried my best to reassure her things would work out, and we'd find a place in which to settle. Home, she retorted isn't a tangible place, it's a feeling, a sense of being whole within.

'Yeah whatever,' and sometimes that girl just cracks me up.

I won't let Angel down, she knows it too. She knows I'm with her every step of the way.

'One for the road, hey Ed?' We are on the same wavelength.

She laughs, 'cause of the situation, 'cause I'm right beside her and I'll never let her fall.

Tim swerves towards the side of the road, taken by surprise as Angel's nimble fingers ease his zip downward and fumble to find his Y-front slit. She nestles her chin up on to his shoulder and whispers something in his ear. His grip tightens around the handlebars. I can just about make out his wide-eyed reflection in the side mirror. Beneath the visor, I'm certain he casts me a wink and I smile back. Enjoy, my good man. Enjoy. The speed bumps add to the excitement of the occasion, the whole length of Warwick Avenue lapped in tar waves.

Frank knew nothing about giving, the only thing Sal got off of him was her P45. It was sent in response to my efforts of blackmail. Poor Sal, turning in her grave, to be still uncomfortable in cold immobility. Freshly deceased and not a tear spilt in her memory. The extremes I have had to go to in order to keep mind and soul together these last six weeks.

If money be the root of all evil, then Angel is the bud about to flower and I the stem. She is my crowning glory. And she is busy so I distract myself.

Money and how to get some, it has been my driving force for so long, the depths I sank to.

Money making scheme No. 1

Hardly worth the endeavour, yielding the tragic sum of minus twenty pounds. Paddington Station, four weeks back with Neville. The aim to fleece the public without seemingly committing a crime, inspired following an emergency visit to the Royal Free.

Phase 1

Neville's scabbed legs were a result of prescription drugs to steady his mental state. They dried his skin and made him itch, and he'd scrape away the top few layers, tearing at the scabs to rub all the harder, sharp pain being preferable to the constant dull itching with which he was inflicted. His legs bore the brunt of his self-mutilation though his elbows were crusted over like patches you sew on worn jumpers. One bout of extreme scraping left him with the bedsheets stuck to his weeping sores. He was in agony, on the verge of derangement, wailing inconsolably for his mother. Poor Neville, and he lay curled up in a ball, his hands clasped tight around his raised knees and rocked to and fro. I ran to his aid, 'Neville, for chrissakes when are you going to get it into your thick skull, the woman is gone. Your mother is dead.'

This served only to intensify his sonorous sobs. Neville was very sensitive on the subject. He chose to believe his mother was with him, kept her room tidy in the unlikely event she'd come back from the grave. It had been three years since he'd waved her off, promising to be a good boy.

The sorry tale of Mrs Bush's demise, unearthed from a chatty social worker who popped round every now and then to check on Neville. Apparently Mrs B, laden down with the weekly grocery shop, had been waddling along the pavement, face down, the rain spitting at her, unaware of the articulated truck bounding down the road towards her. A fatal error made, when she stepped out on to the road to dodge a wide-berthed ladder, then tripped off the pavement, falling prey to the wheels of the truck. Such is life, unjust.

'Leave me alone!' Neville screamed as I yanked the sheet and several scabs from off his legs. He was trembling, fresh blood oozing down his calves.

'Not to worry it will grow back.'

'I hate you.' He began to lash out at me.

The ungrateful little shit. I didn't have to take this sort of crap.

'Hate you too,' and I kneed him in the groin. Neville had the knack of bringing out the kid in me. I hauled him into the bathroom, washed him down, swathed his legs in bandages and then dragged him to casualty.

Sal had had a skin problem, the inability to make her exterior work properly for her. The pores had become enlarged and her insides were apt to dribble out. It was no good, she couldn't mask anything, stress, fatigue, emotional upset, they all showed up on the outside, dark shadows beneath her eyes, twitches, rashes, spots, cysts, dry patches between her knuckles, cold sores. Soft skinned; she once told me in a deadly serious tone that female skin was thinner than male, six layers as opposed to seven.

All the easier to decompose so.

So, there we were, down at the Royal Free waiting for some medically attired person to see to Neville's legs, when I realized how trusting we are of these doctors. How a white coat and identity pin makes all the difference and we impart immensely personal information to some stranger who just happens to be adorned in a uniform. When was the last time you asked a doctor to prove their qualifications? Not that I had any desire to set up a quack practice.

'What do you mean the dermatologist can't see him till next year?' We were at the point of exasperation, having waited three hours.

The harried nurse apologized, dressed Neville's sores and suggested sudocream as a soothing application.

'I pay my taxes . . .' Yeah, yeah, she'd heard it all before as I vented on about it being near impossible to get a decent night's sleep, having to listen to Neville moan in agony.

'We'll go private, we'll sort this Neville, you can trust me.'

Neville grunted apathetically, defeated by his situation. I strummed my fingers on the hospital canteen table, the lunch rush on and a young doctor had hung his white coat on the chair beside us, to bagsy the place before getting his lunch.

Phase 2

One white coat, one rattling bucket, a handful of pebbles tossed inside to give the effect of clinking coins (money begets money) and put the donor's mind at ease. One homemade sign, *Help the Neville Bush Foundation, Please Give Generously*, and the two of us, Neville and myself, circling the Circle Line. We kept our pleas simple and unspecific: 'Children are dying,' we intoned, 'help the helpless to help themselves,' 'The sick need treatment.' 'Give us your money.' 'Fatality affects the aged most.' Obvious and crude but we got the message across and passengers dug deep tossing in their spare change. Without fail, the most yielding of carriages were those with the following criteria: uncluttered, passengers visible to one another, between the times of two and four p.m.

Carriage hopping at station stops and Neville was far from convincing, so I designated him in the role of first benefactor to prompt the other passengers; he'd drop in a fiver and I'd say, 'Why thank you so much, how generous!'.

One woman raised her gaze from the book in front of her and declared, 'I've already given,' but in the main people were fine. 'I don't do charity,' said one, 'Get lost,' another; others expected a conversation in lieu of their copper, on such topics as charity, the health system, weather, or to confess, or in hope of a free consultation and then the woman reading her book looked up at me and snapped, 'For the fourth time, I've already given.'

'It can't be that good.' I indicated to the novel, spread-eagled in her hands; she didn't reply. On our eighth revolvement, my eighth rebuff (okay the bitch was foxy and I fancied my chances), I noticed she hadn't seemed to have advanced much further in the text.

'We meet again.'

'Yes,' she said, laying her book down on her lap. 'My, but you've a big bucket.'

'Loaded.'

'Hmm . . . how much do you reckon you have?'

'About a hundred, maybe two.'

She asked if I liked to fuck.

'Depends on who I'm with.'

I'd said the same thing to a bowler hat and stick, starched shirt of glowing white, with a pink stripy tie which she had witnessed. With charming aplomb he had pressed his card into my hand and whispered, 'Well then, do get in touch.'

She said, 'I think we should, I can tell you're an assertive type.'

I swung down beside her, and we exchanged pleasantries. She had white teeth and a cheerful disposition. I cracked a joke or two, confident I'd bag her later and told her of our mission, she wheedled it out of me. The bucket was heavy and Neville complained he needed to piss badly, so she suggested we get some fresh air, her flat wasn't far from the next station. Thus we alighted.

Fiona Bradshaw, up and coming novelist, travelled the tube pretending to read her book, in an effort to advertise it and raise her profile and she told me she was going to give me the best head I'd ever received. I believed her and she put her hand over mine, clasped to the bucket, and told me I was cute and I'd never forget her. I won't. We were on the upward escalator when she told me to give her the bucket.

'Or what?'

'Or I scream for help.'

And you know what? I knew this wasn't going to end as envisaged. I could see she wasn't joking. It wouldn't have been such a deal if Neville had fallen for her, but it was I who had been duped, tripped up by my own vanity. In the brash, yellow light of the underground, I suddenly noticed all Fiona's imperfections, thick ankles and stocky legs, warthog features and a tic beneath her left eye.

We'd almost reached the top of the escalator when she started screeching for her life.

'They've got my bucket,' both of us pulling hard in opposite directions so I let it go. She went flying and the bucket spilled out its insides, coins and pebbles sent soaring, bringing panic and the escalator to a halt.

'Neville we're out of here.'

'You cunts,' squealed Fiona. It takes one to know one and I grabbed Neville by his collar and we merged with an influx of people, all our hard-earned takings tumbling away. Nev and I switched line and headed back to Kentish Town, where we both got done for travelling with invalid tickets.

Tim is taking his time in coming to a conclusion. Angel too has slowed up for some unapparent reason. Come on girl, keep your focus and the fact is one can't ride a pizza bike with only one hand on the handlebar.

'That's it Angel, think sexy. It will transfer, I mean we're almost there,' almost within sight of Paddington.

'You are not helping Ed,' she mutters.

'Okay, I'll try a little harder.'

Money making scheme No. 2

This episode was fairly distasteful. Okay, so one night I blew Patel (hey, didn't I warn you?). Man, he was always coming on to me and I'd run out of fags. There were two Patels, the grumpy old sod who sold papers etc. alongside his unhappy-looking wife and the flirty, dirty Patel, who was on to anything the minute her back was turned. Patel wasn't fussy, he had a roving, indiscriminate eye, was always coming on to Sal. He'd give her penny sweets with her daily *Guardian* to try and charm her.

'A little bit of sweetness, for a lovely young lady.'

'I'm not that young.'

He'd even asked her out once. 'When are you going to let me bring you out? I want to wine you, dine you, make you feel special.'

Sal would blush, flattered yet disgusted that a leechy old geezer still had such thoughts. I told her to tease him, tell him maybe in another lifetime but her sense of humour had dwindled and she said, he's a Muslim Ed, not a Hindu. Well, my point exactly.

So during my lowest of lows, when every penny had been spent and I'd already cadged a hundred quid's worth of fags off him, Patel proposed a mutually satisfying, business trans-action.

We struck a reasonable deal, a carton of B&H and bottle of whisky for a lick and a polish.

'Open wide,' smiled Patel, as I crouched behind the counter, after making sure he'd turned off the surveillance camera.

'Ohh that's just tickety-boo,' his lyrical accent, setting my papillae on end. Indeed my very tongue fighting for space in my own mouth. Never realized, one could get so sweaty and dirty standing behind a shop counter all day.

And where was Neville?

Standing guard outside the door. He was supposed to have

been my lookout and I'd coached him on intervening at *just* the right moment. Unfortunately, the right moment had already fizzled, having meant to have happened when my head disappeared beneath the counter. I punished him for this later but was relieved when, at last, I heard Nev's dullard tones. He burst into the newsagents.

'She's coming . . .'

Patel nearly had a seizure. 'Who?'

'Have you seen Ed?'

'Go away.'

'But Patel, she's coming.' (And someone would soon, if Neville didn't get it right. Couldn't believe I had spent two hours going over the script with him.)

'Who's coming you dumb shit? I'm in the middle of something.'

'But I think, Patel it's your daughter . . .' I heard Neville dash back outside, then run back in, 'Sorry I'm wrong, it's Mrs Patel . . .'

Man he nearly caught my tongue in his zipper. I, unceremoniously, was booted into the back storeroom.

'Shoo out the back way,' Patel hissed at me.

'The back way?'

'Go, shoo,' and Patel wagged a finger at me, 'Don't touch anything.' And I caught him glance towards a tin box resting on a shelf, he was giving me a hint. I knew it, he wouldn't have looked at that tatty, tarnished tin box if there wasn't something in it. Once, after a hold-up in his shop, when he'd been robbed of a fiver, he'd confessed to Sal that he kept his money safe in an old receptacle you wouldn't give a second glance to, it was there Patel hid all his takings.

So I took it.

Money, just what I wanted, a thick wad of it. That would do very nicely.

I scooted out the back of the shop, met up with Neville, whacked him one, then spent the next hour disinfecting my gob.

In the rear-view mirror . . .

Aghh and Tim's face is tensing up.

Almost there, we fly over the bridge and aghhhhhhround the roundabout.

Tim hoots, you can feel the guy's happiness, it splashes over us, and Angel and I burst out laughing. I don't know why we find it so funny, I guess it's just cathartic, the whole thing, 'cause we're coming to the end of a phase. We pull up at SET DOWN ONLY outside Paddington station.

Tim takes off his helmet and looks bashfully at Angel.

'What was that all about?'

'Oh, I dunno, just felt like it. You know . . . thanks for all your help before.'

'That was nothing.' He's fixated by her. 'No one's ever done that.'

'Well . . . Tim, thanks, I really mean it, thank you so much.'

It's five twenty, it's cold and we have to get going. Goddamn it, it's after five already, we're meant to be at Rob's.

Tim asks Angel if he can kiss her but she shrugs her shoulders and says, 'Let's not spoil a beautiful moment.'

In all seriousness . . . and I tense up again 'cause the morning has rushed up on us and I'm not sure where the night has gone but it has. We disembark and wave goodbye to Tim, hurrying forward into the station. My, my, but haven't they done a lovely reconstruction job here? The station has been transformed over the past few years from Grot Central to Serenity Space, blue neon lights on cold marble paving stones (it looks like marble to me, okay, a cheap form of polished granite), reflective steel and clean glass. There's even a Sainsbury's, and numerous coffee outlets. It's a departure point from which you wouldn't want to leave.

'We need a getaway car, Angel.'

This is uppermost in my mind, we need a car to take us from Paddington to Belsize Park and beyond. Before we rouse Fischer from his hospital slumber, we have to pinpoint a car.

'Shouldn't we just get Fischer first?'

'Angel, he'll slow us down, he'll stick out with his crutches. He'll . . .'

'Angel, Angel . . .'

We swivel round, Tim comes bounding across the station concourse towards us. 'I want to marry you,' he hollers at full volume.

Holy shit and he falls to his knees before her, offering up a sad rose he must have found abandoned by the wayside.

His face is crimson and he begins to stutter, 'I . . . I've never before met anyone quite like you . . . I, I . . .'

Angel leans forward, takes the rose and sniffs it.

'Tim you're a wonderful person but . . . well, I really have to go, it's not the right time or place or . . .' She begins to cry. Okay her eyes water a tiny bit, barely perceptible and there's my Angel, letting him down in the most gentle of ways. Saying goodbye before they even have a chance to get properly acquainted. This is high romance, the very stuff of life and I'm gloating.

You see, what you have to understand, is that Sal would never have done anything like Angel did on the bike. She had neither the nerve nor the guts and curtailed her instinct by subscribing to a set of 'Rules', regarding affairs with menfolk. It crippled her emotionally, all those games and inverted lying. She took it so damn seriously and that's why she lost out. Rob was more cavalier in his attitude, he enjoyed playing with people's heads. Sal would never sleep with a potential boyfriend on the first date, would only ring after a certain length of time. She didn't have the balls to go up to someone and ask them out. Sal lost out on a load of experiences she most probably would have enjoyed and instead held tightly on to the reigns of a self-imposed fake morality. Live a little, I used to nag her, and she'd mock me. Yet there was Tim down on his knees, proposing to Angel and we'd only just met the guy. Sal had ached for a proposal, she'd lay heavy hints at Rob's feet, and he'd dance about her. She tried to get pally with his mother, ringing her up for chats, dinner parties held to impress his friends, bolstering him, at her own expense. She was devastated by their break-up, but she never accepted the reality of the situation, she claimed it was meant to be, that one day, one day he would come for her again and he would urge her to let down her golden tresses. I can recall one occasion after Rob had called round, and in earnest, Sal said to me, 'You'll see, Ed, it's a just phase he's going through, he'll tire of this new girlfriend and come back to me. It's only a matter of time.'

I got the dregs of Sal, the broken, tired Sal, whose youth was fast fading and whose girth had widened. I offered her freedom, she laughed in my face, I gave her unconditional love and she seemed to resent me all the more. Her devotion to Rob never wavered and she blamed herself. As for him, his ego charged up on her, he got off on her. It was hardly his fault women found him so irresistible. He may even have thought he was doing Sal a favour by granting her the odd fuck now and again.

Then there was Tim, eyes glued to Angel, pure puppy worship.

'Angel, can't I come with you?'

'Don't be silly.' She tousles his hair. 'I have to go.'

'I love you Angel.'

'You don't know me Tim.'

He stood up slowly, 'One kiss, please?'

Angel purses her lips and I have to give her credit, she is one sexy lady. Tim's mouth meets hers, he's gentle and sincere. I cough, 'Okay . . . well it's been good meeting you Tim, and you never know, maybe our paths will cross again.'

'I hope so. Good luck,' he says. 'Oh by the way the Heathrow Express is in that direction.' Then he turns, to walk back out of the station.

One wilting rose, early risers beginning to filter through, nightshift workers on their way home passing cleaners on their way to work. The mood is subdued with a clarity of sounds and an uncluttered vision of the short distance.

In silence, we make our way across the station concourse, moments lapsing easily as we walk to the far exit, up the slope to street level.

'Sweet bloke,' I mutter.

'Nice dick,' Angel answers and then announces, 'You know what Ed, I love you.'

We giggle, perhaps it's the fact we're both overtired but something has changed, the urgency of the occasion lifted. During the short walk from the station to St Mary's our pace is light and swift, unforced.

It'll happen, nothing will hinder us. In good time we'll reach Rob's and Angel will let herself into his flat, then Fischer and I will follow suit and . . .

Angel tosses the wilted rose into the gutter.

'It's the thought that counts.'

'My exact sentiments Angel.'

Last Valentine's Day I'd bought Sal a small pot of hyacinth bulbs. The florist promised they would bloom in pink. Sal had been expecting a huge display of floral extravagance. Roses, French tulips, star gazing lilies, orchids. She wasn't impressed by my humble offering. 'It's pathetic Ed, it's worse, it's sad.'

Late, I'd dashed over to the florists during my lunch hour and there were no roses left, the florist suggested I buy something lasting, instead of a bunch of dying blooms. What's more, the only reason I'd bothered was because I knew this type of shit really niggled Sal. I don't subscribe to love being commercialized, if you have an ounce of romance in your soul, any day will do. For Sal it was a huge deal. The tube journey would have been an endless indictment of her failure as a woman if she wasn't loaded down with some sort of material object to prove to the outside world she was, indeed, loved.

The hyacinths were delivered to her office and as far as I was concerned, all was dandy. I sat back and waited for her to show up later at the flat. She trudged home, I spotted her coming from the kitchen window, her face downcast. She disappeared from view as she entered the block. On a previous supermarket shop, I'd managed to sneak in a box of her favourite chocolates and a pricey bottle of wine, just to make the evening special . . .

With trepidation I waited for her, hoping I'd manage to raise a smile to her face. The door opened and she pushed through, looking the most dejected I'd seen in a long while. In she sloped to the sitting room, casting her bag to the floor and slamming the potted plant on to the coffee-table, then collapsed down on to the sofa and burst into tears.

'So, who got you those lovely flowers?'

'Go to hell Ed.'

'Well that's really nice, after all the effort I went to.'

'You sad pathetic spa.'

'I'm glad to see you appreciate my gift.'

'Useless, cringing, fuck-up.'

'Jesus Sal, I thought you liked flowers.'

'Have you any idea how . . . *embarrassing* it was to have a pot of hyacinths delivered to work, not even in bloom, like some poodle flower . . .' She began to mimic her colleagues' remarks: 'Sal, someone bought you a few giant asparagus?' Her voiced was pitched high and squeaky. 'Or perhaps they're some eco botanical toilet brushes . . .' And the entire office had chortled in harmonious unison at the expense of my Sal.

All day she had to listen to their catty jibes. Laughing along with them, to show she didn't really care, what type of idiot would think such a plant could set a girl's heart on fire.

'Oh . . . ha . . . ha . . . yes Ed, I laughed with them and then I said to Carrie, the receptionist, Well, at least I got something. Shut the bitch up for all of a nano second until a courier delivered the most beautiful . . . bunch . . . imaginable. And Ed, I had to sit next to her all the way home on the tube.'

Sal was in floods of tears, choking on her words, snot running free from both nostrils.

'Sal, what do you care what everyone else thinks?'

'A lot Ed, a lot. What's happened Ed? What's happened to me?'

I shrugged my shoulders, as hers rose and fell in rhythm with her sobs. I reached out for a tissue, held it in front of her nose and she blew into it. I wiped the tears beneath her eyes.

'Ed, do you want to listen to some music?'

Man, she was so sad it was contagious and she put on Joan Armatrading. I unwrapped the box of chocolates and ate every one, even the marzipan-centred ones which I hate. Sal uncorked the bottle of wine and glugged it back. She said to me, 'Ed, why was it no one ever wrote a song for me?'

'It's not too late Sal.'

'I've never inspired anyone.'

My God, if she only knew the pleasure she had given when she was a little younger and full of life. Her energy would swoon a room and every ear would try to tune into what she had to say, and if she talked complete nonsense everyone would be convinced that she had uttered something of multi-layered importance. How was it she had no idea of her own beauty?

'No one's even painted me,' she whimpered.

'Sal, come on, you don't know any artists, the likelihood is slim . . .'

'But no one's ever stopped me in the street and said I could be a model or that they wanted to paint me.'

'Don't you remember the time the Spanish guy approached you outside the cinema.'

'Oh yeah,' she gulped back a sob.

This particular event transpired a few years back. Sal had been waiting for Rob outside the Curzon Soho when a man sidled up to her and told her she had a beautiful face and he

wanted to photograph her. He looked slightly scruffy, gave
her his card, said he'd be in London till Sunday and to ring
him the next day. She was, not unduly, flattered. Rob arrived
late, his reaction begrudging and jealously he sneered, 'Was
he blind? Only joking Sal', a put-down followed by a warning
that the guy was probably a nobody who only wanted to
screw her, or any girl, impressed by the presence of a camera
and maybe he was right. Sal shoved the card into the back of
her wallet and forgot about it till months later when, flicking
through *Vogue*, she came across a huge piece on the photog-
rapher. Juan Whatever was having an exhibition in Paris and
was unanimously considered the Man Ray of the late
nineties. One of the bylines ran 'turning Paltrow down'.

Sal snivelled, 'Oh yeah. I forgot about that.'

'See Sal, you've had loads of opportunities, you just blew
them all.'

'But hyacinths . . .' she sighed, like it was the end of the
world.

'If only you'd listened to yourself . . . Sal, you could have
been immortalised in negative form.'

'At least on Valentine's Day Rob bought me roses.'

Conversations always had a knack of coming back to Rob.

'Only out of guilt and a day late.'

'He was busy, he forgot what day it was.'

'He was busy screwing the pop star.'

The final Valentine's Day they had officially been
together, Sal received a very large bunch of red roses,
twenty-four hours late. And I mean colossal, easily two
hundred quid's worth of blooms. At the last minute Rob
had called Sal and cancelled their arrangements. He was
producing a music video for a pop babe, a screeching
Finnish cocktail of exotic genes, mixed race, some would

claim 'genius', and the shoot went over time. Pissed off, he told Sal he'd pulled the short straw and landed the job of having to take the elf out and entertain her. 'It's business,' he assured Sal, 'work, you know I'd much rather be with you. I'll make it up to you. Promise.'

Five o'clock, next morning, in the Siren's room at the Covent Garden Hotel, Rob rubbed open his eyes to see his Northern Star pack up, she was leaving to catch a flight to New York. Her room, heavy scented, was packed full of flowers and off the cuff she said to Rob, 'You have a girlfriend don't you?'

'Yeah.'

'Take these.' She smiled, offering him a huge bouquet of red roses. 'Thank her for the loan.'

Rob caught a cab back to the flat, snuck in, showered quickly, then presented the arrangement to Sal and to add a touch of romance later that morning they stopped off for breakfast at Amato's in Soho for the best pain au chocolat in London.

Sal was thrilled, too easily pleased, despite the fact the card was addressed to *My northern light long may you shine, love your greatest fan, Dan*. She didn't put two and two together. Never even suspected, merely assumed it had been adorned with the wrong card.

It was me, who eventually felt duty bound to enlighten Sal, pointing out that on the songstress's second album, a critical success though commercial flop, 'Roses For Rob's Girl', third track down, spelt it out cruelly. The verse lyrics went like this: 'for a bunch of red roses, I am northern light, in London town, screwing around with someone else's man, 'cause I can' (heavy upward emphasis on the last word).

'See, Sal you have been written about.'

'Indirectly, you know what I mean Ed.'

'What? That it's fine to screw you over as long as he buys you flowers.'

'It's the thought that counts.'

Sal was exhausted from all her sobbing and the bottle of wine and I realized it would have been futile to carry on the argument.

'Exactly.'

We turn off Praed Street and the mood shifts up a gear. Nearing the main entrance of the hospital Angel and I are impeded by the presence of a police officer doing his duty on the lookout for suspects, suspiciously like ourselves I don't doubt.

'How are we going to get Fischer out?'

'Leave it to me,' she says, confident in her disguise. 'Have faith, I'll slip in with some nurses . . . don't worry something will turn up.'

We watch as the officer paces outside the main door, obviously bored out of his skull. Minutes tick away, nothing happens.

'Maybe we should call Fischer, let him know we're waiting.'

'And wake up the whole ward?' Angel shakes her head, 'We've just got to be patient.'

'Was that a joke?'

She sneers, 'Come on, we aren't going to blow it now.'

Yeah, yeah keep the faith, a little patience is all that's needed. We remain hidden from view.

'I need to piss Angel.'

'Snap.'

'Copy cat.'

Whatever I do, Angel wants to do it too. We wander around the side of the building and find an enclave in which to relieve ourselves. Half crouching, watching the steam rise as the night's fluid splattered against the wall. We pace back to our original position, the cop is chatting to a patient, having a crafty fag outside.

'You find us a car and I'll get Fischer,' announces Angel.

Of course it'll be better if she goes in alone, together we'll stand out. The cop is bound to ask questions if we appear, fitting the brief exactly.

'You think you can get by him?'

'Look it's my problem Ed. Nothing for you to worry about,' and I can tell she's trying her best to reassure me. 'You sort the car out and if I'm not back in twenty minutes come and get us.'

'You sure about this?'

Having marked out our territory, we arrange to meet back at 'piss-point'.

Aw shit and I mean, the fact was, the situation didn't bode well, what the hell did I know about hotwiring cars, *nada*. I should just ring Fischer, I'm thinking, I should just do it. It was sweet of Angel to offer and all, but she really wasn't up to the job. One thing at a time, the least I could do was let Angel have a try, you never know, she could well succeed, though I have to admit I severely doubted her chances. I needed a smoke or some kind of diversion and reached into the pocket of my jacket. Out popped a golden nugget of technology. A GPRS mobile, a very nice diversion, I must have picked it up at Imelda's, the Aussies and their love of all things techno. I'd no recollection of taking it. That's how trusting they were, so blasé with their valuables, 'cause they could always be replaced from the seemingly bottomless pit of one's parent's wallet. Well, if they would be so careless

Piss Point

and I thought I'd connect up to the net, see what power this little motherf. would yield.

It's a bloke thing, you know a form of escapism. On I clicked, remote access status connected and I fiddled in a text message and after a couple of minutes this was what came back: . . . a picture of a lady with dick up her ass . . .

As if, come on, do you think I'd waste precious moments, do you really think so little of me?

This is what came back: 'Raw Data for Raw Nerves', 'Getting in Cars the Easy Way'.

Isn't technology a beautiful thing? I scrolled down the tiny text, trying to take it all in. The requirements kinda bothered me, an accomplice (another reason to have kept Angel with me) a clothes hanger and getting the right wires fused together. But all surmountable, how hard can it be, and as I read though the text it mentioned the likelihood that some idiot would have left the car door unlocked, even more likely, I thought, a stressed idiot who'd arrived at the hospital all of a fluster.

So off I trotted in search of badly parked cars and a certain type of idiot.

Out on a limb and I'm such a dork, Fischer would most certainly know how to hotwire a car. So stupid, I'd have to hang round for twenty minutes, hoping Angel would be able to rouse him.

'Aw man this sucks,' repeating Neville's exact words to me, the night he kicked me out of his flat.

The night Coleen and her boyfriend arrived at Sal's old flat and discovered the state it was in. Neville had been all distressed, going on at me about how I took advantage of him. The very night I realized it was time to go. Spread my wings and fly, fly, fly, but to where, I hadn't a clue. Realized too late the reason one maintains close friendships, for the good times and the bad times. Neville's kitchen clock ticked me off. This was a bad time. Okay confession, Sal was my only friend, I'd killed my only friend and there was no one to turn to in my hour of need. We had become mutually dependent on one another. After her break-up with Rob, the fact gradually sank in that she too had lost all her friends in favour of his. That's how we found ourselves alone. She had invested everything into that relationship, had hung out with his crowd, forgot to nurture her own friendships so when the split occurred they didn't want to know. A dumputee, her social world concaved, she found herself in the pits. Thank God for video stores, late-night shopping and evening classes. Yes a few attempts were made to re-establish old ties but people had moved on. Poor Sal, tried her hardest not to be cast out from the trendy fold of Rob's world but they treated her like she was a traffic light window washer, and sped off into the distance of acquaintanceship. She'd call to ask what was happening and they'd answer in vague terms and make excuses or cruelly tell her outright that they were Rob's friends and their loyalty lay with him. So when I showed up, she was all for it, a little desperate and perhaps I took advantage of her in the given situation, but the truth was she wouldn't have cast me a second glance if things had been different and I seized the opportunity. I moved in on Sal, we hung out and it would have been fine if Rob had only left her alone, I wouldn't have had to kill her.

The night I quit Neville's, he told me I could keep a spare set of keys just in case I couldn't find anywhere else to stay.

'Nev, thanks for everything you've been a true mate.'

We slapped shoulders, hugged at arm's length, the English way of men.

'So this is goodbye Ed.' Neville sniffed, uncomfortably formal.

'Yep catch you later, nutter.' I winked at him. It was time I ventured forth, besides I had no desire to run into Coleen and Roger.

Where to?

Well, where else but the production offices. Sal had a key, I'd kept all her keys. Her P45 had arrived in the post that very morning. A visit to the office had the potential to yield further possibilities in my attempts to blackmail Frank. A conclusion I reached, after wasting an hour and half in Tower Records in Camden. Frank was proving to be a real bugger. He really didn't want to part with any of his cash. I caught a bus into town, the offices situated near the Telecom Tower, off Tottenham Court Road. I hadn't been there for a long while and prayed no one would be around, working late. I used to collect Sal from the office when she was doing overtime, so I knew the entry code. I let myself into the building and trudged up three flights to the office. Luckily it was empty, I surmised the cack documentary must have been in production and they were off shooting shit. Eerie inside, the office was snoozing, the fax machine kicking in every now and then, but nothing much had changed.

There was Sal's desk, though all her stuff had gone, (her red stress ball, signed autograph picture of Vanessa Felch – *Be good to yourself Sal, love V. Felch* – and her novelty burger eraser). In their place were photos of a kid with heavy-set glasses. No visible sign of Sal remained. I rifled through her old drawers, slightly miffed as her replacement appeared to have slotted in with the greatest of ease. To be fair, the filing was in top shape, neat, accessible, whereas Sal was apt to have bits and pieces of paper strewn everywhere, in a chaotic system that only she could access. Sal could have learnt a thing or two from this new woman. It saddens me that people by and large are expendable. Each of us unique but for what purpose? A maudlin moment and I sat at Sal's old desk, clicked on her PC and went through the e-mails, ascertained the replacement's name, Sindy, a single mum (internet history showed up sites such as onyerown.com and all4acouncilflat.com). I skimmed through her files to pry at what had been going on in Sal's absence. Sure I could have trashed the place but why? Whatever I decided to do would have to urge Frank to gladly part with a lot of dosh.

Noreen Sheedy woke me up.

Noreen was a strange kettle of fish, a sour, disgruntled woman, embittered by life, she worked as a cleaner in the production offices and had done for the past twenty years. Sal and herself had got on fairly well, they passed each other on a daily basis, Noreen about to clock off and Sal to start her day; if time allowed they sometimes stopped to moan over a morning coffee.

'Bejayus Mary and Josephine you nearly had me heart stopped,' she screeched, spying me slumped over the desk.

Her mother had come from Ireland and her father, a Scot, had been a Royal Merchant Navy Seaman.

'In the name of God . . . in God's name . . . what do you think you're doing?'

Shit, shitty, feeling heavy from the lack of good sleep.

She had a fair few whiskers on her chin which she teased at, as I spluttered out the reason for my presence. The moving plight of Sal and the desperate predicament she found herself in, her pregnancy and Frank's reluctance to do anything about it, how she'd lost her job and flat. Noreen offered to make us a cup of tea, 'There, there . . .' she clucked, 'that's nothing compared to what's been happening to me.'

'What's that?'

'I tell you that Frank has it coming to him,' Noreen sniffed, and confided how only the other day he had taken her aside and spoken about the golden age of advancing retirement. 'It's time you put your feet up Noreen, he says to me, the cheek! Pastures new, like I'm a fecking cow.'

'How can he be so callous?'

'He's a bastard is what he is.' Noreen shook her head in dismay. 'I'm a woman in me prime, you know, one day it will be time for payback.'

The sooner the better and I wondered how far Noreen's anger at Frank would extend and if we could amalgamate forces and teach him a lesson.

'I want Frank to give Sal some money, is that terrible Noreen, is it so bad?' I admitted to her how hurt I was about it all, Sal was in dire need of financial assistance and Frank, well he'd hardly miss the money.

'Money?' Noreen shrugged the suggestion off. 'Frank's notoriously tight-fisted, you haven't a hope in hell!'

'But together Noreen, you and I, if we could come up with some way of getting at him.'

'Blackmail the bastard, is that it?'

'It'd be worth your while, I'll give you a cut of whatever we manage to get.'

'A percentage of the profits?' Her eyes began to sparkle at the thought. The pittance of her pension was all she had to look forward too. 'I could take a holiday.'

'You could Noreen, you could do whatever you wanted.'

'After all my years of service you know what? . . .'

I interrupted her flow, 'Noreen would you help me, I mean, help me get back at him, for Sal, for the baby?'

A heart the size of a schooner had Noreen (we're talking sherry but at the time I was misguided, assuming ship, more of that later . . .), anyhow my spirits lifted and we set to conspiring.

'It's a delicate situation, he's a difficult man. We'll have to outsmart him, what had you in mind, what exactly are you proposing?'

Well that was it, I shook my head, I'd not an inkling of how to go about it. 'Would you?'

'No, no I don't, to be honest I wouldn't have a clue, but I'll have a hard think.' She left me sitting at the desk, rubbing my hands over my face, the vacuum cleaner burst into action and she nuzzled her way in and out of desks, sucking up the dirt.

I'm still not sure when the idea struck, whether it was over by the photocopier in the corner or outside the gents' toilets. Anyhow about five minutes later, the vacuum cleaner hose turned upright and Noreen Sheedy hollered over to me, *'Eureka!'*

Wonder of wonder, miracle, miracle, because my hand presses down on a Honda hatchback handle and the door begins to give.

Thank God for idiots, where would we be without them?

Must have tried fifty cars, have slipped round the side of the hospital to a small car park backing on to the canal. The driver's seat is covered with a wooden ball, back massage device, a two-inch religious scented icon hung from the mirror, St Cecilia if I'm not mistaken, an angel playing an organ. There's a Bible on the passenger seat and cushions in the rear. Then I see it, a white rat jumps up at the window, my stomach lurches with it. Red eyed, long tailed, I have a thing about rodents, they freak me out, freeze me up.

'Get away from my car!'

A large Caribbean woman yells at me, she comes waddling over. 'What you doing at my car?'

Get me out of here. She carries a shiny hand bag, raises it as a shield, up to her voluptuous chest.

I gulp, the rat scratching at the window, and queasy at the mere sight of it manage to mutter, 'Admiring your rat.' I can see its teeth.

'You tink I'm stupid?'

She's three feet from me. A sister off duty.

'What you doing here? This is a staff car park.'

Swinging her bag towards me like I'm a flea. She has reduced me, reminds me of a teacher I had. The mind is so trained in its reactions, a constant let-down. I could have pulled the gun on her but I'm stuck in a long lost moment of childhood humiliation. She clatters me one across the head.

My but she's huge, imposing, pointing her finger.

'I'll get you arrested . . .'

'Honestly, I used to have a rat as a kid, I noticed it jumping about. Came over to have a look.'

Liars always give too much away.

'So you like me rat?' This person grabs my arm, opens the car door, the rat jumps on to my shoulder.

'Say hello Snowy.'

'Hello Snowy.' A feeble hollow utterance hisses from out of my throat.

Every hair raised as I feel its snout ease under my collar, its small furry body, claws and all, following suit. I so very nearly shit myself, will do, if I don't concentrate on keeping my hole clenched due to some Freudian instinct.

The lady, see how polite I've become, wedges herself inside the car and it sinks with her impounding weight. She whistles and ratty climbs back up my torso. Jumps into her arms as Caribbean lady glowers at me. 'Waste of space. You should be ashamed of yourself.' She slams the door, then drives away.

My head hangs low, not may I add from shame, but because the meatballs I'd consumed earlier are having a second outing.

Man am I pissed. How come I'm not as invulnerable as I thought. And where the hell is Angel? I should have put my foot down, we should never have split. From the corner of my eye I notice a security guard approaching.

'Oi woss goin' on?'

Vomit splatters, what the . . .

'You alright?'

'I'll be fine, I'll be okay . . .' I stammer.

He puts his arm around me, not aggressively I must state, but comfortingly.

'I was just . . .'

'Come on, we'll get you seen to.'

'Yeah, I don't feel so good.'

He escorts me to A& E, back past the piss point, a quick glance confirms my suspicions, no sign of Angel or Fischer and it must have been near on twenty minutes since we separated. I'm in the reception area. I've done it, made it, oh for silver linings.

'We'll have you sorted in a jiffy.' Why is he being so kind? 'You've a lovely smile,' he adds for good measure. So that's it,

I must be his cup of tea and he goes to get me one from out of the machine.

'Best be off, some one will be with you in a minute.' He hands the plastic cup over.

'Cheers and thanks.' Christ the man even winks at me.

'All part of the service.'

Hands in his pockets, back through the automatic doors.

What happened? Is there a hidden lesson therein, the sweetness of the tea calmed me. The guard had calmed me. You know, I quite liked him.

Now I just have to find out where Fischer and Angel have got to.

Sat on a plastic chair, sipping tea and a couple of drugged-up prostitutes perch down beside me.

'What you looking at?' Her face is hard, embittered, I mean really hard with lesions, she probably has aids, her companion wears the same look. They're sub-strata human.

'Fuck off.'

I haven't said a word, not a thing.

'What?'

'What you gawping at?' Her eyes are on my bag. Then, their pimp arrives, exactly as you'd imagine, swarthy, small, talking on his mobile phone. Those people they would have eaten the rat, they would have bitten its head off.

'Oiiiiii,' she gives me a dead arm.

Three against one, the forecast isn't good. I've been here before, if they're after a fight they can look elsewhere. The pimp takes my vacated seat.

'Don't mind her, she's had a rough night.' Well haven't we all.

Their eyes are dead, their whole demeanours boarded up,

saying 'don't touch me', strange for whores, surely a contra-
diction in terms?

'Not a problem,' and I walk away.

Ward 3B, third floor up, that's what Fischer said, that's
where I head, too much time spent faffing outside. I should
have strode straight in. I hear the women cackle loudly as I
move away, even the sound of their laughter is forced, no
humour in it at all. Sal was jelly in comparison, wonderfully
soft she was, vulnerable sure, but celestial compared to those
human crusts.

Maybe I should have saved Sal.

The Save Sal campaign, as conjured up by Noreen Sheedy,
office cleaner, and undertaken by our good selves, in the
effort to blackmail Frank.

'*Eureka!*'

Noreen stood with the vacuum nozzle hoisted up and
shrieked across the office floor to me. 'Ed, I have it.'

By Jove but hadn't she only come up trumps. I couldn't
hear a word the woman was saying until she switched the
machine off.

'So what do you think?'

'Run it by me one more time.'

'Frank's reputation, remember the story, the one with
the courier, he's never lived that down and under the present circumstances, I'd be surprised now if we couldn't
persuade him that a buy-out would make good business
sense.'

So we conspired to lay a trail of conscience jabs before
going for his jugular. Jabs and subtle pricks, over the course
of the next week the following occurred.

Tactic One

To get Sindy (his replacement P.A.) on our side, I typed up a documentary concept and left it on her desk – 'Fleeing responsibility' an in-depth look at fathers to be, who fail to take responsibility for their offspring. She would read it, and impressed by the content, would present it to Frank as her own idea, eager as his new assistant to please.

Tactic Two

Junk Facsimiles, Unfair Dismissals, Have you or do you know anyone who has been unfairly dismissed? Contact: Solicitors, Doody and Brookworth.

The above tactics worked on a subliminal level, the two concepts easing into the subconscious, getting ready for the coup d'état.

Tactic Three

Mis-sent e-mail, unfortunately to the office gossip, the gob that couldn't remain shut, that flapped constantly. Marked VERY PRIVATE AND CONFIDENTIAL, its purpose to raise an eyebrow or two.

Dear Frank,

I beg you to reconsider, why won't you speak to me, when you know you are the father of my unborn baby? All the promises you made, about divorcing your wife and then you send me my P45. I don't understand why Frank. When you said you loved me I believed you, why are you doing this to me? Please tell me this isn't happening . . . I love you Frank and our child needs a father.

All my love,

Sal xxxx

For a quid I set up office in Easy.everything, down at Charing Cross. I received the following reply,

> Dear Sal,
>
> You poor babe, your e-mail came through to me by mistake, we are all really concerned. I hope you don't mind but I told some of the others. Frank had told us you'd let him down badly, chucked the job and gone off somewhere. What a bastard!
>
> Love,
> Monica
>
> P.S. if there is anything we can do to help, just let us know.

Bingo! This was obviously the way forward.

> Dear Monica,
>
> Thanks for your email, I can't describe to you how upsetting this all is for me. He won't even talk to me and I really don't know what to do. It's all so confusing. He's sacked me Monica and doesn't want anything to do with me. I know it was really stupid to have an affair with Frank but I really fell for him.
>
> Love,
> Sal

> Dear Sal,
>
> Hang on in there, we're all on your side, Frank is being a right tit about it. Everyone now knows. How come you've moved? I called the other day, the woman who answered went off on one, I think they

think you trashed their flat or something, all very
strange, then they said, if you see her, tell her she's
dead. So I'm worried about you Sal, where are you?

Love,

Monica

Dear Monica,

It's such a complete mess, the landlady evicted me for
no reason whatsoever and I haven't a clue about the
woman who answered the phone. Oh Monica, I really
thought it would work out with me and Frank, and I
know he must be under loads of pressure, but
everything has come tumbling on top of me, losing
the flat, my job, the pregnancy, to be honest I feel
suicidal.

Love,

Sal

Etc. etc. tongues got wagging, the news spread like foot and
mouth, Sal firmly established as the victim. Noreen reported
back daily shifts in office tensions and all behind Frank's
back, until that is, the office arselick, the brown-nosed slime,
asked Frank if he could have a couple of words with him.

'I thought you should know Frank the troops are disgruntled, there's talk of . . .'

'Spit it out.'

'Well, the business with you and Sal.'

'What's that?'

'You sacking her 'cause she's pregnant.'

'What?'

'And now word has it she's homeless and has attempted
suicide.'

'Who knows about this?'

'Everyone.'

At this point Noreen intervened. 'A shocking disgrace, is what it is, a man in his position could be so callous, you know what Monica, the whole office should rebel, demonstrate, mount a campaign or better a very public collection.'

'Hmm . . .' Monica pondered, quite a good idea, if only she'd thought of it. The adoption of other people's ideas as one's own is a common policy, especially that of a perceived underling. A chance to play the good Samaritan, thus the Save Sal campaign came into being. Via an office e-mail the plight of Sal became public. A picture of Sal was scanned into the computer with the dates of her office life imprinted below. Unfortunately, it was a rather hideous image, she'd been snapped, red-eyed, totally plastered and from a terrible angle, double chin and forced Cheshire grin, taken at last year's Christmas bash. The wording ran:

> As most of you know, due to unfortunate
> circumstances our esteemed colleague Sally is,
> sadly, no longer with us. She gave her all to her
> job, was punctual, reliable, honest and above all
> loyal. A bright, vital and funny woman with a
> unique, self-deprecating sense of humour she is
> sorely missed. As a mark of respect to our dear
> colleague, we shall be holding a small drinks
> ceremony in the local this lunchtime, where a
> collection will take place.

I'd no idea Sal was actually, well, really liked. The staff rallied to her cause and Frank began to wilt visibly. He couldn't help noticing the catty remarks and gestures, the dirty looks, the fact that the entire staff, en masse, appeared to have taken Sal's side.

When asked to contribute to the collection, Frank's face almost curdled in panic.

This had to cease, the whole company would crumble, his status was in jeopardy. The democracy of spirit, the fact that people power does make a difference, democracy does exist (so I urge you people . . . use your vote), and the timing, coincided with the office's busiest period. Frank feared a walkout, a strike, he felt uneasy in his own business. He confessed all this to Noreen, who had found him slunked in the sofa, the one where waiting clients usually sit, the one where he and Sal had screwed.

'I suppose you've heard,' he sighed heavily, his shoulders bent inward, 'about Sal and me.'

'Who hasn't?' replied Noreen, sitting down next to him and patting his limp hand in hers. 'Before you know it Frank, it will be all over town, might affect your business reputation. You'd want to sort it out, I've heard nasty rumours, some of the things they're saying about you. It's shocking.'

'I've made a mistake Noreen . . .' Out splurged his sense of helplessness and the initial blackmail tactics but most importantly the fact he felt ridiculed.

Now Noreen was smart, she appealed to his inflated ego. 'Frank, get rid of the cow. I always knew she was trouble. Take my advice, you want her off your back and if I were you, I'd consider a pay-out. Cut your losses and have done with it, what's a few grand to you, a man of your stature, come on Frank, you can't let something like this undo you.'

'She's asked for thirty thousand pounds.'

'Crikey and what are you offering?'

'Ten . . . look I've no proof I'm the father.'

'But Frank, the cost of childcare these days . . . it's phe-nomenal.'

I'd spent the entire week sleeping in the office, sneaking in after everyone had gone. Noreen would wake me in the morning and fill me in on what was happening. So the next day, after her tête à tête with Frank, Noreen arrived in jubilant spirits.

'Result,' she yelled, rubbing the palms of her hands together.

Well what do you know, but things were beginning to happen, at last.

'Yippee Noreen, we're going to be rich.'

The office box was tuned to MTV and Britney, one of Sal's idols, broke into *I was born to make you happy*. I wrapped Noreen in my arms and we copied the video dance routine. Sal used to do it pretty good, she had gone to great lengths to get the dance steps right, purchasing a teenie girl mag which had come with diagrams and free plastic hair clips. I was to call Frank later that day to discuss the pay-out.

Man was I relieved, the breakthrough I'd been waiting for, the things I could do with all that money.

'Thirty thousand, just think Noreen . . .'

'Frank seemed to think ten was more appropriate.'

I stopped in mid twirl, was she for real?

'Achemm.'

I swing round.

Angel appears in front of me.

'Where the hell have you been?'

'Fischer's not in his bed.'

'Immaculate powers of observation Angel.'

Ward 3B, the pair of us stand outside, Tweedle dum and Tweedle dee, and Fischer isn't snuggled up in his bed.

'I've already checked the toilets.'

I'm getting pissed off with this, we're losing vital time and against all odds, having managed to get to Fischer, the Slavic Shit isn't there. His bed covers tossed aside. He isn't there.

'Where the hell is he?'

'How would I know?'

'You incompetent, he's gone!! Where's he gone?'

'Don't start on me Ed, I'm not in the mood.'

And hey, it's always easier to take it out on your nearest and dearest. I swing round, storm back to the lifts, my teeth clenched in rage.

'This place stinks and Angel I knew you wouldn't be able to find him.'

'You know what Ed, you really are your own worst enemy.'

'Thanks for the vote of confidence.'

'We're running out of time.'

'You think I don't know.' I spit out the words, they dribble down her chin.

'Ed, if you keep this up, you are on your own.'

'What a jerk-off, can't believe I trusted that scuz.'

'Ed, you really don't know how lucky you are.'

Angel always looks on the bright side of life.

Lucky! Well that shuts me up, not because she's right. Sure I'm lucky to have her, to have a future, rat scratches on my back and a tingling arm; no, my jaw's gripped tight because I think we've reached the end of the line.

So this is it, without Fischer we're screwed. Our plan well and truly rendered obsolete, next time I see that guy, I'll break his other leg.

'I'm going to kill him.'

'Who, Ed?'

'Who do you think? The least you can do Angel is keep up.'

'I'm not carrying Rob's death on my conscience.'

'Who asked you to?'

How come hospital lifts always take forever? We're back at the lift, waiting for it to take us down to ground level.

'He's round here somewhere. I know it, I just know it.' Angel sniffs the air like she has a heightened sense of smell.

'I don't care, Fischer's blown it.'

'I reckon he's either looking for us or has been arrested.'

'I've had my fill of Fischer, I don't want to know.'

Just like Rob, constantly letting us down, falling way below expectations.

'Angel, from now on I refuse to deal with this kind of shit.' Same old, same old, you want something done.

'What are we going to do now Ed?'

I snap back at her, 'I'm thinking. Goddamn it, I'm trying to think straight.'

What to do to salvage the situation when the plan had been so perfect in its conception.

We ride the lift down to ground level, the doors part and we barge out, no sign of the copper, maybe they've taken Fischer in for further questioning, maybe there's a man in the moon. My lips purse in anger and then Angel goes all biblical on me: 'I was thinking along the lines of Samson and Delilah . . .'

'Nice one, so we go give Rob a haircut. I mean that's well hard Angel.'

'I'm only trying to help.'

Rob's hair is curly, he's blessed with a full head of it, no receding hairline or emerging bald patch. We'll need a razor, we can do his eyebrows too. At least it will ruin his big day and embarrass him slightly.

'Look Ed, I know it's kind of juvenile but it's something.'

'We could cut his ear off.'

Reservoir Dogs, Mr Blond and the cop. Man, I got off on that scene, I mean what does that say about me. Steelers Wheel. *An' I don't know why I came here tonight, got a feeling that something ain't right . . . clowns to the left of me, jokers to the right, here I am, stuck in the middle with you.*

Apt or what?

'Ed, the ear thing, I don't think I could go through with it. You know how I am about blood.'

Can't stand the sight of it, poor Angel, liable to faint, maybe the hair thing is the right way to go . . . and then . . . as if we weren't already in enough trouble . . .

We cross over the street, fury driven when . . .

Arghhhhhhhhhhhhhhhh . . .

Caught in freeze frame by a gut-wrenching howl, like an animal in mid maul.

Arghhhhhhhhhhhhhhhhhhhh . . .

The van beside us, parked half on the pavement, is the source of such ominous emissions. My first thought? I really don't want to get involved.

The driver's door swings open and there wedged between the steering wheel and seat is a woman on the verge of dropping her load. Her face contorted in fear and agony.

'Help . . .' she pleads, 'it's coming.'

'Don't even think about it Ed,' Angel pre-empts my reluctance.

Christ someone else is bound to hear her, we're only a couple of hundred yards from A&E.

'Ed, don't you dare,' and already Angel is releasing the seat back, allowing the woman to slowly ease down out of the van.

And I haven't a clue how she managed to drive herself to the hospital in the first place.

'I'm sorry,' she's sobbing mid contraction. 'It wasn't meant to be like this.'

Damn right it wasn't, none of this would have happened if Fischer had turned up when he was supposed to. How could he? In the name of God I had trusted that man. The whole thing would have been over, we'd have left Rob's, there'd have been no messy situations, no Gloria, no hubby, no itchy scalp due to the shitty wig.

'Angel would you just stop scratching for a minute?'

Arghhhhhhhhhhhhhhhhhh . . . Poor cow, doubled over in pain, her cries piercing the early morning calm and you know what? I know exactly how she feels, she's the physical manifestation of what's going on inside my head, right at that moment.

Arghhhhhhhhhhhhhhhhhhhhhhh . . .

'For God's sake Ed, give her a hand.' Angel rebuking me, the woman in squat position, I hand the bag over to Angel, then bending behind the woman, I slowly ease her up.

'Okay lady, you think you can walk a little?'

We inch forward, Angel cooing words of encouragement, 'It's going to be fine, just fine.'

'Oh God, oh my, oh God, oh my God.' The woman in quite a state, Angel hollering at full volume, 'We need some help here . . .' or words to that effect.

'It will be okay, breathe in, breathe out.' Heck, what do I know about childbirth? 'Where's your partner?' There I am, attempting to make idle chit-chat.

'A Goddamn bitch with a turkey baster,' she bellows.

Oops.

'Just a few more steps lady, come on, you can do it.' Quite a few, but help is already on the way in the form of the security guard who emerges from his security hut and comes sprinting up to us.

'All right love, we'll have you sorted in a jiffy.' Together we haul her up the winding slope towards A&E. She's on the verge of another contraction.

'Drugs I need drugs.'

Don't we all. 'Arghhhhhhhhhhhhhhhhhhhhhhhhh.'

A bit late for that I'm thinking.

'Take a deep breath darling, you're doing fine, you're doing brilliant.' The guard's voice soothing and effective.

'I'm scared, Boo-Boo, I'm scared . . .' She's talking to her stomach.

A nurse meets us in reception with a wheelchair, the whores and pimp exactly where I left them, still waiting to be seen and as we ease the woman into the chair, doesn't she only go and foghorn holler, 'The keys . . . I've left my keys in the van.'

The guard throws me a sidelong glance, 'cause the pimp's ears have pricked up and I guess they must be regulars.

'I'll get them, I'll be back in minute.' Angel bends down and kisses the woman's forehead, 'Good luck.' We turn round and make a dash for the door.

'Angel, manna from heaven.'

'Okay Ed, but promise me, you'll return it.' And you've got to respect Angel, she's a moral creature after all.

Yep she's on my side and the pimp is breathing down my

neck. He sidles up right behind us, his flick-knife reflected in the glass of the doors.

Okay . . . let's just slow things down a bit here.

'Easy does it.' And for purposes of practicality I'm going to call this guy Ahmed, we never do get on first name terms. The tip of his blade pushing through the layers of my clothing, its tip tickling my belly.

'Keep walking.'

I catch a waft of his aftershave, if I run for it, the blade will sink further in. It was a good manoeuvre on his part.

I point to the car, 'It's over there.'

'Yeah?' Ahmed isn't sure if he can trust me, 'What about that one?' There are two vehicles parked on the street, one at either end, does he really think I'm going to point out the wrong one and then make a run for it?

Yep and yeah I have, 'Okay it's the large white one.'

'Ow.' The knife sinks a little deeper, grazing me. 'You sure now?'

'Certain.' Besides, the car is clamped.

'No funny stuff, you get me.'

Damn, 'cause right at that moment, you know what? I have a great joke about a bartender and parrot I'm dying to share. So we cross over, retracing earlier steps and where's the police when you need them . . . gee this country is going to the dogs. Ahmed prods us forward all the way to the van.

He lets out a low whistle. 'A transit van, my lucky night.'

Come on, come on, I want this incident closed, get in the van and fuck off out of my life. Just take the van and leave us alone. A lot of money is riding on this, all I ever had. We had, are likely to get and my logic is to comply with the geezer.

'What's in the bag?' enquires Ahmed.

*

'Ten grand! A measly ten grand?'

I had called the office the day Noreen told me it was time to negotiate. Frank's opening offer and I laughed out loud, roared contemptuously.

'That's a joke right Frank?'

'Not until I get proof I'm the father.'

'I thought we'd already been over this?'

So Frank had balls and was about to call my bluff.

'You know what Frank, maybe we should just let this come out in the open. It's going to cost you a lot more in unfair dismissal: "Boss Sacks Former Pregnant Employee Carrying His Love Child". The tabloids would go for it. I've no doubt about that.' Well maybe if Sal had been a bearded midget lady and Frank had a humpback. I was desperate.

A long pause followed.

'Listen Frank, why don't you have a little think and I'll call you again tomorrow at three.'

'You're a dirty cunt.'

'Whatever.'

As I'd invented the whole thing, Sal now a phantom with a phantom pregnancy, I didn't have that much room in which to manoeuvre, a compromise would have to do. I reckoned that all the after-hours work Sal had put in would most probably have amounted to ten K. Frank was getting off pretty lightly, then again, I wasn't in a position to refuse, besides I was sick to death of being broke and kipping in the office overnight.

The next day at the assigned time, I called Frank, he sounded happy which irked me.

'Ten grand take it or leave it.'

'Fifteen.'

'Ten,' and he wouldn't budge for an age, I guess that's why he's so successful, business being in his blood.

'Look Frank, the bottom line is, how much do you value your reputation? For my part I've promised to get the staff back on your side and I will.'

'Eleven.'

'Frank be reasonable, I know where your kids go to school. Listen, do you want me to go stand outside the gates and introduce them to their half-sibling.'

'Eleven.'

'We'll call it quits at fourteen and you won't ever see or hear from me again.'

'Twelve.'

'Thirteen.'

'Twelve and that's it. Thirteen's an unlucky number, we don't want the kid to start off on a bad omen.' He snorted with glee. 'My final offer.'

'Twelve it is.' The deal done, and a long time coming, five weeks to the day.

Noreen was in raptures. 'Six thousand pounds!'

'Excuse me?'

'Fifty-fifty, as agreed.'

Had I really? I'd no recollection of that decision. I'd thought she'd have been pleased with about two.

'Noreen, now I don't want to fall out with you but . . .'

No buts and she told to me to cop on to myself. 'Fair is fair,' she said. 'After all it was my idea.' And she scoffed at me, 'Thirty K, you've a cheek, there was me expecting fifteen and you can't even manage to swindle more than twelve. I wouldn't have bothered if I'd known it would be for so little.'

Well that put me in my place. Anyhow Noreen agreed to

act as a go-between. We worked out the finer details, Noreen would collect the package and bring it to me at a designated place, I'd check it over and then for my part resurrect Frank's reputation via an e-mail copied to everyone in the office.

The smell of money and I was reeking of it, counting it out note by note. Frank kept his word, handed over the package to Noreen, who I'd arranged to meet in the all-night snooker hall down in Holloway. Now call me hyper-suspicious but I wasn't going to take any chances. I wouldn't have put it past Frank to have Noreen followed, or follow her himself.

I lurked by the side of the office waiting for her to appear. Sure enough when she emerged through the revolving office doors, Frank was by her side. She put the envelope in her everlasting shopping bag and stuffed it into the top of her old lady trolley, then turned down the street toward the bus stop. A second later, a middle-aged bloke in a donkey jacket emerged out of a Ford Escort parked by the side of the road, motioned to Frank and began to follow in Noreen's footsteps. Aha, a private Dick, explaining Frank's previous good mood on the phone. I fell in step behind him.

Then get this, a bus pulled up, Noreen jumped on board, Donkey Jacket after her and I broke into a canter to try and catch up, but the bloody bus moved off before I could get on. The reason I'd lagged so far behind was because the bus was headed in the opposite direction to where Noreen was supposed to be meeting me. Turncoat. Now that really wasn't on, to be double-crossed by the cleaning lady, and after I'd agreed to her cut in the first place.

So I stood cursing her, but the thing was, how far could she plausibly get. When she failed to make the delivery, the Dick would get suspicious and she'd be left with nothing. The next bus arrived, I stuck out my hand, paid for a ticket and sat up the front end. Obviously Noreen was unaware of the fact she was being followed. It made sense, from Frank's point of view there would have been no reason to involve Noreen in his duplicity, unless he was paying her off, but if that had been the case she would have come straight to meet me. Anyhow the bus trundled along, one stop further and I noticed the bus in front had stalled and spewed out its passengers who were now clustered on the pavement, all of them hoping to catch the next bus. The one I had boarded.

The bus pulled over to the stop, Noreen stood in the centre, clutching the handle of her trolley, Donkey man to her side. The crowd began to pile on, I was staring at her through the window, she glanced up, caught sight of me and winced. I smiled at her, like it wasn't a big deal that she happened to be travelling in the wrong direction. She boarded the bus, waved her pensioner's card at the conductor, the Donkey man pressed up behind her. An overcrowded single-decker and there were cries of 'move down along the bus,' as more people shuffled on.

There I was, sat in the seat reserved for the feeble and elderly. I tapped Noreen on the shoulder, 'Here lady take my seat,' and bent in further to whisper, 'Don't say a thing, we're being followed,' as Donkey man wedged into the row of seats opposite us, at a ninety-degree angle, facing us, while we looked ahead. Noreen sank into the seat, there was enough room to push her trolley in by her legs. I clung to the handle above, my back directly blocking the Dick's vision and as the bus moved off, I jerked forward. 'Plainclothes cop, Donkey jacket, thank God you changed route.' I could see the envelope sticking out of the bag. Noreen's lips curled inward, she wasn't sure who to suspect, leant back in her chair and caught Donkey man's intense stare. I mouthed the following, 'Fucking Frank, double-crosser.'

The bus lurched to a sudden stop.

'Give me the envelope. It's our only chance,' I murmured across to Noreen. 'I'll leave the money in your bucket tomorrow.'

It was winking at me, a plump, brown, padded envelope. My hand reached out for the package, her fingers met mine and I thought I heard her suppress a yelp. 'Trust me, tomorrow, six grand. I promise.'

Noreen let me take it and I pressed it tight to my chest and at the next stop disembarked from the bus.

Noreen, Noreen, oh you silly woman, I was so disappointed in her, she'd blown her chances, had had me willing to give her money. In the situation she had to trust me, it was all or nothing, if the package had led the Dick to me it would all have gone straight back to Frank. The shock on her face, a final glance back, deep shock and perhaps a touch of bewilderment, such a shame, especially considering all her hard work. Twelve grand the richer, all for me, money and the things it can do to people. It's a human reductive, brings out the core essence, the original smell.

And of course, as a thanks to Frank, I kept to my side of the bargain and issued an e-mail that would get the staff back on his side.

Dear Frank and everyone,

Thank you so much for all the money (12K plus the collection which had amounted to £300, pretty

impressive I thought). Anyhow I know you are all
going to hate me now, because the truth of the matter
is I'm not pregnant nor was I ever, but I do have
personal problems if that's any consolation to being
shafted.

I'm sorry about this. No really I am and if I ever
get a chance to pay you back one day, I promise I
will.

Thank you so much for all your generosity,
especially you Frank and of course Noreen.

All the best,

Sal

I mean, to have seen the look on everyone's face, man what
I would have given. Twelve grand in my hand and I pressed
SEND.

All that money and all mine, mine mine. . . .

It happened so quickly and I'm not certain of the sequence of
events but, the next thing is Ahmed pushes Angel up against
the van. Man this guy is sleazy, his upper lip sweaty and he
grips Angel's face with his free hand, smarming at her, 'You're
quite a looker . . . we could have some fun.'

Angel spits back at him . . . her gob splattered between
his eyes. He slaps her hard across the face, then rips the bag
off her shoulder.

No way, there's no way he's having the bag, there's no
way and at this juncture I'm going to explode, Goddamn it,
God fuck, is this some kind of karmic kickback, you win
some you lose some, what comes around goes around, you
know Saturn's up my anus and Pluto's having a good old
laugh 'cause the money, our future is slipping away.

Ahmed opens the door, slams it shut, the ignition starts, the engine hums, Angel and I gobsmacked, pounding on the window, 'The money, the money, **YOU FUCKER**.'

Our fists thump against the side of the door as the van slides off the pavement, down the road, the pair of us pathetically running after him, till rasping for breath, hands on knees, I pant,

'Angel, what happened?'

'Ed, I guess . . .'

'Angel . . .'

'Ed,'

'Angel,'

'Ed,'

Angel Ed Angel Ed Angel Ed . . .

'It's over.'

All that money, all gone, gone, gone . . .

Over, it was over and who'd have seen that coming?

End of Story

Not quite.

I whimper, 'No, no, no,' three barely audible no's, eked out.

I mean, I never got to tell you the interesting stuff, how I met up with Fischer or the plan, or . . .

'Ed . . .'

Leave me in my misery, leave me wallow, for pity's sake . . .

'Ed . . .'

. . . half expecting a fat slag beneath a lamp-post to burst into song . . .

'Ed . . .'

. . . my self to combust and innards sprawl over the pavement . . .

'Ed!'

'What is it Angel, what . . . what . . . what?'

'Look.'

In the near distance, can it be . . . can it possibly be . . . the car appears to be swerving over to the side of the road, there was a screech of tyres and then it jolts to a sudden stop.

Angel and I doublesprint, one–two, one–two, one–two and we get to the van and as the windows are dark, we can't see a thing. I yank open the front passenger door.

'Edwards, what took you so long?'

Fischer was pressed up against the back seat, his sock wrapped around Ahmed's neck, throttling him, the guy's face purple, his body kicking out like he's having a fit.

'Angel, nice hair.'

'Thanks Fischer.'

Smiling at each other, the bag flung on the passenger seat and I reach in, take out the gun and whack Ahmed across the side of his head, knocking him unconscious.

'What do you reckon we do with him, Fischer?'

'In the back, time ticks.'

Fischer . . . How can I have doubted him, after all we have been through together, are about to go through? I knew straight off we were kindred spirits, both dislocated, in limbo, waiting for the next turn of fortune.

His eyes are a dark blue, I dunno, maybe he wears tinted lenses, they're pretty intense, framed by black lashes and he's got Slavic cheekbones, a strong nose, high brow and black hair. Angel thinks he's the bee's knees, when she came to on his sofa, after the fight, the first thing she said to me was, 'Christ Ed, he's beautiful.'

I sighed, 'I wouldn't know.'

Early thirties, a six-footer, broad shoulders and lean torso and he wore pressed white shirts beneath a suit, like he was a somebody, plus a golden smile, not to mention a wife and kid back in Moscow.

Boris Fischer.

'Where the hell have you been?'

'Waiting for you.' Like it was my fault. 'You always late, it's prerogative, yes Angel?'

'I'm not in the mood.'

We drag the slumped-over Ahmed from the driver's seat and shove his body into the back. I take out the binding tape and wrap it round his ankles, wrists and mouth. The guy is out for the count.

I stretch up my arms, fingers interlaced, my knuckles clicking. Ahmed lies curled up in the back, Fischer has moved to the front passenger seat and Angel is watching me from the rear.

'Ed,' she says, 'Ed, I think you're amazing.'

I mean, times like these, that's the sort of thing you want to hear.

'Christ that was so close. I thought we'd lost everything.'

'Me too.'

I slam shut the back door of the van and climb up into the front. I can still smell Ahmed's scent on the seat, the keys have fallen from the ignition during the scuffle down at my feet. I pick them up, edge the seat forward, then look at the time, it's 6.30.

'We're cutting it fine.'

Angel giggles, 'Ed, was that intended as a joke?'

Nope, more an oblique double entendre as to what's coming.

Fischer turns to me. 'You know how to drive truck?'

'Seeing as you're out of action I'll have to give it a go.'

His right ankle is in plaster and he's dressed in hospital pyjamas, faded, tatty and a woman's dressing gown.

'Don't you have any crutches?'

'I dump them.'

'I'd given up on you.'

Fischer raises his eyes at Angel.

'I thought yes you have.'

'So where the hell have you been?'

He says he'd been keeping watch all night, looking out the ward window every half hour, hoping to see us down below.

So he was peering out, caught sight of us emerge from the piss spot and decided it would be best to go downstairs, try to meet up with us there. Only by the time he managed to hobble down we were nowhere in sight. He cadged a fag off the copper and stood outside a while, must have just missed Angel on her way in, while I was contending with the rat.

He continues, 'Went back inside, if cop thinks it strange for me to stand there. He tell me he go off duty twenty minutes. Do I go back to the ward or wait? This is my dilemma. Then, Edwards, (He calls me Edwards, like I'm a plural), from the corner of eye, I see you with security guard. I not convinced, if this good or bad. What should I be doing? I wait in gents toilet. I hang, try imagine what you think and stay for bit. What does Angel do in this situation, yes?'

Angel's knees turn to jelly, she digs his accent, his low tones and slow deliberate speech.

'Huh? So there, that Edwards, is where I am.'

'Was,' I correct him.

We're travelling five miles an hour as I do my best to get to grips with the van. A glance in the rear-view mirror catches Angel twiddling strands of black hair, twirling them round her finger, almost flirtatiously. I guess she's warming up for what's about to happen.

We move out on to Praed Street.

'Any music? Fischer, see what the woman has.'

A shitty radio, Fischer twiddles the knobs, backwards, forwards till we hear *You're Once Twice Three Times a Lady* and I can't suppress shaking my head in disbelief.

Jesus but Sal really did have cack taste in music, no really.

Sal's all time top three.

Number three. Magdalene's 'I don't know how to love him' from Lloyd Webber's *Jesus Christ Superstar*.

Number two. The Communards' cover version of 'Don't leave me this way.'

Number one. Well you've guessed it, 'Three times a lady', Sal's number one favourite tune of all time is the very song playing on the airwaves, so apt it's as if it had been pre-dedicated.

'Know what Fischer I was ready to kill you.'

'That's what I think. Edwards going to have guts for garters.'

Fischer's sense of humour is somehow enhanced through translation, he continues with his story.

'I leave toilet, go outside, see you, the truck, hear scream and watch you drag woman over to hospital. I witness whole thing, very helpful Edwards, show you have heart. I had doubt but you surprise me.'

'So then what?'

'You left door open, I know you come back. You go in with security man, I get in truck. Then you exit with creep and I watch careful. I know is not right. I watch fight, take off sock, and when he starts driving, *ghhchucct*!' A guttural sound squeezes from his throat and his hands mimick the attempted strangulation. 'And now we are happy, no?'

Once more I shake my head, the guy is unbelievable.

'But we together, no?'

'I'm happy,' chirps Angel.

'Yes, it all good,' and he brushes his finger down along her cheek.

Fischer came out of the blue, at a moment of incredible need. After I'd embezzled all that money, I reckoned I deserved a treat, for a start a full-size bed having suffered lower back pain from kipping in the office. I headed straight for the

Savoy, Sal had always fancied the Savoy, she preferred old-time glamour to the hard aesthetic cool of contemporary times, all minimalist with a couple of white lilies thrown in for good measure.

One night when we were tucked up in bed together, all warm and cozy, she sighed languorously in answer to my question, 'My favourite fantasy Ed? A huge bed with heavy, clean, white linen, a bottle of champagne, perhaps some tasty tidbits, you know finger food, and I'd have had an all-over body massage, facial, leg wax, the works. I'd be smooth, blemish free, toned up and I'd smell edible, like people would want to stand closer to me in an elevator just to get a whiff. Oh yeah, I'd recline back on the bed, in a silky number, flesh protruding in just the right places, fashion mags strewn all over and then reception would call and announce, 'your guest is on the way', and well . . . guess the rest.'

I obliged her request, sarcastically: 'There's a knock on the door and Rob comes in, you make mad passionate love. He proposes and you spend the night in a state of bliss.'

'What about you?'

'I'd like you to be happy.'

'Bastard. You always have to go ruin everything don't you.' Disgusted by me, for I had snapped her back to reality.

So, I checked into the Savoy, I did it for Sal, right after I'd sent the e-mail through to the production office. I would have given anything to have been a fly on the wall, to have witnessed Frank's expression on discovering he'd been had. He'd had Sal and I'd had him, that's the way it goes. Third floor up, suite 116, black and white marble tiling and mirrors, all art deco and curvy wood, not to my taste particularly and I rang down to reception and ordered up a bottle of champagne and full body massage.

Within five minutes Robin came rapping on the door. I'd just stepped out of the shower and answered it with a towel wrapped round my middle.

'Hi, I'm Robin.' Blond curly hair framing a sweetly cherubic face greeted me and gently nudged me aside, the equipment heaved through the door, ready to be set up in the living quarter of my sumptuous suite.

'How do you like it?'

'Hard,' I answered.

'I have lots of oils.' Robin remarked, putting up the massage bed.

'Great.'

Another knock on the door and room service arrived with a bottle of champagne on ice.

'Put it there, please.' I pointed to the dressing table and gave the maid a quid.

'Are you ready?' quipped Robin. Sure was and I climbed up on to the bed and lay belly down, my face poking through the hole.

'Would you like me to put on some comforting music?'

'Sure that would be good,' and then I surrendered to those all-powerful hands.

'My, my, but you have been stressed out,' Robin informed me with genuine concern.

'To the limit,' I murmured.

Teasing out my knots, fingers digging deep. For the next half hour nothing was said, as hands pummelled my back and shoulders, then worked on my toes, ankles, shins, calves, followed by large sweeping movements, up to the top of my thighs. Robin flipped me over on to my front and asked, 'Would you be interested in any extras.'

What could that mean?

'How much?'

We discussed figures, mine, Robin said, was lovely. 'Yours,' I replied, 'are exorbitant.'

We agreed on a number and I lay back to enjoy the ultimate in room service.

This was more like it, I thought, enjoying the experience, being attended to in such a manner.

'Is this good?' asked Robin.

'Aghh . . . very.'

Sal had it all wrong, this was luxury, total pamperdom and after we finished, I offered Robin a glass of champagne.

'Just a small one, I've another client to see.'

'Shame, it would have been nice to hang out for a while.'

'I'm free later. Call me on my pager.' We left it at that.

I lay down on the bed, warm and aching from the release of the session. Sal would have been disgusted, she'd have accused me of exploitation, denigrating my fellow man for my own sexual pleasure.

Had I degraded myself? Surely not and Robin left happily enough with a wad of my notes. On the contrary, I felt it was moral behaviour, I had responded positively to a proposition that was up front and clear in its intentions. Perhaps, if Robin had been a woman, it would have felt different, but seeing as he was a baby-faced Muscle Mary bent as a hunchback I'd harboured no seedy connotations. I mean, I hadn't got off on dominating him, in the sense of having paid for him. I did not harbour the implication that I somehow could do what I wanted with him, that he was within my power, no he had pleasured me and had provided a much appreciated service. Besides, I had been the one in the physical position of submission, splayed out on the massage bed. Anyhow it beat having a facial.

I overindulged my senses for the next day and a half, restricting myself to the pleasures that exist momentarily and catered to those visceral desires, high-class hunger (oysters, caviar, foie gras), lubricious substances, the best chateaux swam down my gullet, 100% pure Bolivian coke sucked up my nostrils, loved up on Versace E and a bit of GBH. My feet never touched the ground 'cause I rented a stretch limo with a couple of pole girls thrown in for good measure. I'd rung one of the city's foremost gentleman's clubs to employ the services of two of their finest dancers for an evening of pure pleasure. Initially they thought my request odd and then threw in a bouncer for free, just in case I got touchy feely with either of them. So the limo pulled up outside the club, whereupon Barry, Jan and Tina emerged from the side of the building and climbed into the back with me.

'Ohhh nice interior,' mocked Barry and I pointed him to the front passenger seat.

'You, my good man, must travel up front.'

He wagged his finger at me, 'Any funny business and I'll have you.'

Yeah, yeah, I turned my attention to the pair of rented lovelies beside me: 'Well . . . hello girls.' Patting the empty seats, I urged them to submit their fine arses to the leather and indulge in spirits of their choice.

Jan and Tina had come decked out in sparkly, itsy-bitsy bikinis and very high heels. They were both striking looking with, one must concede, perfect bodies to whack off to, though their faces were camouflaged in a ton of makeup.

'So what do you have planned?' trilled Jan, 38, 26, 38, curvaceous lady.

'Anything particular in mind?' giggled Tina, 36, 24, 36, grrrrrrrrr . . .

'To show you two girlies a good time. Help yourself,' I smarmed, offering them lines of the white lady. My desire was not carnal, rather it was to indulge my sense of potency. A club crawl with these two lovelies dancing around me. I'd agreed they could keep their knickers on, wanting them draped over me as accessories. You know: to objectify their sexuality, after all that was their trade, but they refused to play the game and started going on as if they were at a coffee morning and what jerks men were.

'Look darlings, I didn't pay to hear your opinions.'

'What are you like!!!' They were taking the piss.

We went to a couple of clubs and they did what they were told but rather half heartedly and I could see they weren't taking the evening seriously, blah, blah, blah, 'It's us that's got the power, I make £250 on an average night, you should see the state of some of the blokes, my God . . .' The pair of them nattering on about women's issues, girly stuff and if I had to listen to another catty comment about sad wankerdom, I'd have flipped so I hurled them out on to Leicester Square at 3 a.m. and went back to the Savoy alone.

Cast to sea on a linen cloud, the bed's too big without you Sal and I was missing the intimacy of a naked body's warmth and steady pulse entangled with my own. I began to understand better the type of loneliness Sal must have felt and her inability to cease grabbing at the scrap-ends thrown to her by Rob. My mind was wired, jaw unhinged, not a chance of sleep and for the next few hours I thought about Rob and what I could do with him. My mind racing, his impending marriage, my own future, the past, the night I did what I did to Sal. The sense that she was still with me, her spirit lingering on, Frank and the money, Noreen's face as the bus moved into gear and took off, the smell of Imelda which had lodged in the back of my throat. Overcome by a sense of floundering and then finally, sleep.

Next day I took stock of the situation, realized I'd already blown quite a big hole in my takings, almost two grand, time to downgrade. I stuffed a couple hundred quid in my pocket, checked out of the Savoy and left the backpack, containing the rest of the money in Charing Cross Left Luggage. Later that day Neville called me on the mobile and suggested I come over. There were no other pressing arrangements so off I trotted back to where I'd hailed from.

That night I sampled GBH, only the real stuff this time, actual grievous bodily harm. The night of the fight, Kentish Town farm when I came face to face with my Angel.

He'd sounded a bit preoccupied on the phone, not his usual happy go lucky self and when I arrived up at his, he ignored me for the first five minutes.

'You're not here Ed.'

'Eh, okay whatever.'

About turn and he began making out he hadn't called me, saying I should go and you know, I'd kinda been looking forward to seeing him, I even considered paying the bugger back some of the money I'd scabbed off him.

'Ed, you're not a real friend.'

'Nev, you been watching Oprah again?'

'If you were, you wouldn't have pawned all the stuff you gave me.'

Christ an assertive Neville, something had got to him.

'Okay what's eating at you?'

'Yeah and you never did one nice thing for me.'

So not true. Had he forgotten our minor adventures, the

trip to the hospital, the tube fiasco, Patel the prick, the hours wasted hanging out together? Hadn't I shared my company with him for nearly three weeks?

'Name one thing Ed, one nice thing?'

'The boat trip, the day we sailed down the Thames.'

'You know I have a phobia about water.'

'Yeah but I was hoping to cure it.'

So perhaps I'd abused Neville's hospitality but I did bring him on a Thames cruise. It was the day of the tube strike and London Travel were offering free boat rides along the Thames during peak travelling hours. It was an opportunity I couldn't miss out on and I dragged Neville along, down to Tower Pier where we embarked on an Absolute Pleasure Boat with three hundred others. Sailing up and down, Neville seasick from the motion and the crush of people and okay I admit it, it was a total disaster but the intention was honourable, to do something different. We jumped off at Waterloo, walked back over Charing Cross Bridge and I treated him to a McDonald's.

'Hey and you got a free action Ronald McDonald in your kiddie box.'

'But Ed, I'm a vegetarian.'

'You're too damn fussy, you won't get anywhere with an attitude like that.'

'Ed you should go.'

'I'm not going anywhere, I came over specifically to see you, at your request.'

'I didn't say anything.'

'What? You're not making any sense. Are you on new medication?'

He pointed to his bruised eye.

'What happened?'

'Aw forget it, just go.'

But I stayed, having discovered his new prescription of mind-altering pills, and then the pair of us headed off down the Prince of Wales Road to Kentish Town farm.

Chasing the sheep and I could hear him bleating, 'You bitch, you bitch . . . ED!!'

Whack . . . what the . . . serious tripping and you already know what happened.

The night I met Angel and scrapped her off the shitpile, man my head was done in. Then Fischer stepped out of the blue like some fucking Prince Charming.

'Where the hell have you been all my life?'

Neville had fled from the scene of the crime, skedaddled, you know I had my suspicions, reckoned he set the whole thing up.

A small cul-de-sac of houses backed on to the Kentish Town farm and it was from one of these that we were spotted. Fischer later told me he'd been taking a pee, had looked out the window and saw the whole fight or most of what had happened.

Ain't there always someone watching, isn't that just the truth, particularly in this city. Fischer said at first he thought we were kids, messing around but as he shook the last drip from his dick, he realized something was seriously amiss.

So he came and rescued us. An Angel in my arms and he scrambled over the wall to where we were.

Earlier in the evening he had picked up a young couple in the West End and gave them a ride home, discovered they were ex-Soviets and a common bond was formed, a drink offered and he partook of their hospitality until his bladder reached bursting point. He excused himself, which led him up their stairs, into their bathroom and offered him a spectacle he did not shrug from.

He tumbled upon us.

'Help,' I squeaked, Angel falling in and out of conscious-ness and somehow we managed to drag her back to Fischer's car, past the slumbering animals penned in for the night, and out into the street.

He drove us back to his place in Finsbury.

'Good luck – I'm a doctor.' He informed us, putting on the kettle to sterilize a needle. 'Fischer, my name is Fischer.'

'Ed, Angel,' I murmured, stunned by what had occurred, the ferocity of events unfolding, the fight, Angel and this man, appearing out of nowhere. My mind spun out, laying Angel down on his sofa, he checked her torso, in case any ribs were broken, cleaned her up, placed a pillow beneath her head. He threaded the needle and I held on tight to her, as he bent down over her, to stitch the gash above her eye.

'You will be okay,' his voice reassuring. 'You know, we have saying . . . there is fable in Russia about two brothers . . .' and as he gently punctured Angel's skin he began the tale.

There were once two brothers called Ivan and Fydor. Ivan was full of goodness whereas Fydor was full of evil . . .

Fischer broke off from the story to tie a knot in the thread, pull it taut and then bite it. Angel whimpered, tensed up and then sank back on to the pillow. Fischer stroked her brow, his face close up to Angel's and he remarked, 'Beautiful eyes . . .'

Cringe and I'd a good mind to stick my fingers down my throat and barf. I mean how cheesy was that, as good as, 'do you come here often', but Angel's lids fluttered and she later told me, he had gotten away with it 'cause he'd sounded sincere. Anyway back to the brothers, awaiting the redemptive bit.

. . . Fydor grew rich and old and when the time arrived for him to die, he travelled to a warm land with three servant girls who tended to his every need and though he was a hated man, he did not care, for he had led the life he wanted and he died in a large, comfortable bed with clean sheets, attended by the youthful and beautiful.

'How bad?'

. . . As for Ivan, the older he got, the poorer he became, his acts of charity went unrewarded, all his good deeds were easily forgotten and he died in a mental institution, unkempt, uncared for and alone.

Pupils darted randomly beneath Angel's eyelids, falling into sleep, her hand, which gripped mine, loosened and I snuggled tight beside her.

'But the point?' I murmured. 'What is the point of the story?'

'Shit happen . . .'* concluded Fischer. 'As you say, roll with the punches.'

Jesus was this guy some type of comedian?

I fell asleep on Fischer's sofa, wrapped around my Angel.

We woke late the next morning, Angel real sore, the smell of freshly brewed coffee came wafting from the corner of the room. My eyes slowly blinked open and I could see Fischer over by the small stove, bare chested, standing in his trouser bottoms.

---

* I have an inkling Fischer regarded himself as something of a Chekhov protégé, nosing through his stuff I came across a drawer of stories, essays, poetry, etc. He caught me at it and said if I was interested I should check out his website. [Shit Happens. The Fantastic Fables of Boris Fischer available on www.fabfischer.com]

'You want some coffee?'

'Mmm . . .' My body seemed to creak with every exhalation. I must have drowsed off, I vaguely recall lifting my lids once again to glimpse Fischer ironing his shirt and then, when I finally awoke, the place was empty. Just Angel and I trying to put together what had happened the night before.

Fischer lived in a crummy bedsit, strictly speaking a studio as it had the added bonus of a minute shower room and toilet, overall a dismal habitat. He'd left a clean towel on the small circular table with a note, 'Angel, Edwards, I work till 9 p.m., please be home and see you later. Fischer. PS Help yourself.'

In former days, the bedsit must have been a living room. It was large, high-ceilinged with double windows looking out on to the rear of the house; a junkyard, a mass of weeds and overgrown foliage. He kept his room tidy, didn't have much personal stuff, a small bookcase, makeshift wardrobe. There were a couple of photos of his kid on the mantelpiece over the defunct fireplace, a small two-bar electric one in its place.

Angel didn't say much, the battering had left her stumped and her mouth was twice its normal size. I pulled myself up, my legs jelly and went to take a shower.

King of the road, a white transit van cruising along, myself at the steering wheel while Fischer sits staring out the passenger window.

'Edwards, we are nearly there?'

'Yeah, just about.'

'You are certain you want to go through with it.'

'Excuse me?' Like I would have put myself through all this hell to bail out at the last moment. I don't think so.

'Angel, you are sure now?'

'Fischer, like I said, I didn't come this far for the ride.'

I sneak a glance at Angel and she winks back at me.

'What about you Fischer?'

'Please don't worry about me.'

Sal used to say she missed having someone to worry about, that was one of the worst things, no one special to focus on and care for. Maybe that's a key difference between the male and female of the species, in that most women inherently find it easier to sacrifice their self, their ego, this being a requisite of motherhood. Perhaps it isn't an innate female trait, it may be due to conditioning, circumstances or whatever. Fuck I'm no sociologist, but I do know that when Sal hit thirty, her sense of the passage of time heightened and, most importantly, her realization of her own mortality. Her belly ached with emptiness, it wasn't as if she had an amazing career, oodles of cash, material goods or even a hectic social calender in which to distract herself from herself. By the time I got to her, she was lost in her own personal haze, emotionally crippled and stinking of desperation.

You know the type, strung out on their own sense of failure, and I'd catch Sal beating herself up, putting herself down and you know what? I'd join in.

I regard this process as a natural human reaction. 'A.' likens herself to shit and pleads to be treated in such a manner whereby all others comply to the letter. We tend to believe one another's prognosis. By the way, I'm six foot four with a ten-inch dick.

So what exactly does this say about human behaviour and the natural inclination to distance oneself from one's fellow man when he/she is weak, failing, depressed, desperate and therefore, by default, most needy? Is it our fear of contamination, of being brought down too? (Just a thought.)

Anyhow, in the end I was so full of contempt for Sal, her final shred of human dignity snapped the day she called round at Rob's. The day I did her in, it seems like ages ago, a lifetime.

You remember of course, it was the morning after Sal found out Rob was engaged to be married. The morning after the night he'd called round to the flat and screwed her, she was bulging out of that dress. So damn tarnished, I could hardly bear to touch her.

She'd smoked a whole pack of fags till nauseous. She tossed and turned, then crawled out of bed and ran over to Rob's, hoping to persuade him of God knows what; to take her back? not to marry? to declare undying love? to walk all over her after she'd thrown herself at his feet? One or all of the above, and off she went in her altered state of mind.

The woman was in a frenzy, she actually ran all the way from Kentish Town to Belsize Park. A spare set of keys jangling in her pocket, she'd kept them after the split, according to her logic they represented a link to the past and her future. Rob had forgotten all about them and she failed to remind him. Anyhow, when she reached Rob's, her face drenched in sweat and tears, she let herself in, through the main door of the house converted into three flats, flung herself up the stairs, then began pounding on the door.

'Rob?' wailed Sal, 'Rob I've got to speak to you, Rob, Rob . . .'

'Who is this?' came an unfamiliar voice, in reply to Sal's hysteria.

'Rob, Rob I've got to speak to you'

'What the . . .'

Sal was screeching, 'Let me in Rob, please . . .'

It was seven and she was standing in her ex's hallway. It never once occurred to her that she could still turn back, it wasn't too late, but oblivious to this she continued sobbing solidly, 'Let me in. Let me in.'

The door opened and Justine appeared wrapped in an old towelling robe of Rob's, one Sal had bought for him. Sal hadn't expected his girlfriend to open the door. Stunned into silence, she stared at Justine; in her imagination Rob would have opened the door, but there stood Justine in his place, younger than Sal, with long, wavy, dirty-blonde hair and the first thing to strike Sal was that Rob's fiancée bore a slight resemblance to herself. Only when she was younger.

'Where is he?' Sal shrieked, pushing past Justine, 'Where is he? Rob? Rob?'

She ran into the bedroom, the room she'd spent nights in, the bed she'd shared with him, the bed empty and she was squalling like a wounded animal, pulling the sheets off the mattress, 'Where is he, where is he?'

Justine was shouting, 'He's not here.'

Sal rushed at her. 'What have you done with him?'

She kept repeating the phrase, till the second thing to strike her was Justine's palm and it took a few moments before Sal felt the sting of a sharp slap across her face and collapsed on to the floor in a heap.

'Is Rob here?' Her voice was all choked up.

'He's at the gym.'

Mondays, Wednesdays and Fridays Rob went to the gym. It had been that way even before Sal. Wednesday, of course he was at the gym, she'd have to go, to the gym. That's where she'd go.

Justine helped her to her feet.

'You can't marry him, he doesn't love you,' Sal blurted to an unsuspecting Justine.

'It's okay Sal, just calm down.'

'He doesn't love you.'

'Okay . . . Sal please calm down, take a few deep breaths.'

'Rob, I'll wait for him,' she wailed, as a young child's plea, all sense of reason having departed from her.

'Rob's going straight to the office from the gym.'

Justine, to her credit, tried hard to contain the situation.

'Rob said . . . look Sal, I know he told you last night we were getting married and I'm sure it's a big shock . . .'

'He told you?' Sal gasped.

'Yeah, last night. He told me he'd called you.'

'You know about Rob and me?'

Justine stared at Sal in a pitying sort of way, just like you'd regard the loser of a race, the one who came in last. She winced at Sal, hoping not to exacerbate this picture of derangement in front of her. As tactfully as possible, Justine said, 'I know Rob still means a lot to you.'

Sal stared blankly at her. 'You do?'

Justine nodded.

'Really?' Sal quizzed.

'The phone calls Sal, remember? '

Sal, it must be mentioned, had sunk lower than low, calling Rob at various times, essentially to hear his voice and then she'd slam down the receiver or blast out a long list of profanities if Justine answered. This had continued until Rob changed his number, so, in spite of herself, she'd then taken to sending letters, long love letters to Rob and, receiving no reply, had sent through hate mail addressed to 'Rob's Bitch'.

Justine smiled awkwardly at Sal.

'You know about Rob and me?' Sal reiterated.

Justine shrugged, 'Yeah, of course.'

'Don't you mind?'

'It's none of my business.'

'You don't mind?' Sal gawked at her, disbelievingly.

Justine handed her a tissue, to wipe her eyes and running nose.

'You know, we're still sleeping together.'

Justine pushed her hair back off her face, embarrassed now and wanting Sal out of the flat, her sympathy drying up.

'Rob said you'd say that.'

'Last night we slept together.'

'Listen Sal, you should go now.'

'Last night, he was inside me when you called.'

'Okay Sal, whatever.'

'You've got to believe me Justine, I swear to God.'

Justine's mouth contorted as Sal continued. 'He called round to see me Justine, he didn't call me.'

'Sal, I know you're going through a bad time but I think you should leave.'

'I can prove it. You called when we were making love.'

'Time to go Sal.'

'Half nine, you called around half nine.'

Justine made no reply, doing her utmost to guide Sal towards the door.

'Feels Like a Woman' was playing . . . you know the song, 'this is a man who needs a women . . . I'll never be unfaithful,' and God love her but didn't she only try and sing a few bars of it.

'For fuck's sake, just go now Sal.'

'He doesn't love you . . . he never loved you.'

'Sal, I'm trying to be helpful here . . .'

'Got a few loose ends to tie up,' Sal repeating the exact phrase from Rob's conversation of the night before.

'Okay Sal, that's enough.'

'Justine, we've been together the whole time you thought you were his girlfriend.'

'Get out.'

'He loves me!'

Justine stared at Sal.

'OUT,' she screamed, forcibly pushing Sal out of the flat, back into the hallway. 'Get out now.'

Sal spat out the following, 'Almost forgot, Milo's offered us his villa in the Bahamas, we'll talk about it later, love you Angel,' doing her best to mimic Rob. 'We were together last night, can't you see, it's me he loves . . . Me.'

Shards of the telephone conversation, exact and precise, Sal had gotten to Justine, the truth sprinkling down on Justine, trickling through and, unable now to contain her anger, Justine yelled, 'He feels sorry for you Sal. He calls you his psycho.'

'Liar, he loves me.'

'Out. Now.' This was not a request, Justine shoved Sal back out into the hallway, then slammed the door in her face. Worse thing of all though, having shamed herself so appallingly, Sal bent down and shouted through the letterbox.

'I'm Rob's Angel . . .'

You'd have thought she'd have dragged herself home, tail between her legs but for the next ten minutes Sal remained hammering on the door, her heart splintering, fists clenched, face streaked with rage screeching,

'I'm his Angel . . .' over and over until the police came to pick her up thanks to Justine's invitation.

Their presence shocked Sal back to some level of sanity and a policewoman, highly trained in diffusing the emotions of overwrought females, helped Sal down the stairs and offered her a shoulder to cry on.

'Come on love, things aren't that bad.'

Oh but they were, indeed they were, and Sal was escorted home in a police car, all the neighbours twitching at their nets, to see who was in trouble this time.

How could she? I'll never forgive her, never understand how.

Angel thinks I was too hard on Sal.

'You were too hard on her Ed, no one's perfect. The word is almost redundant, meaningless, nothing is ever perfect.'

You know there was a time in my life when I believed in perfection, that things were fundamentally right or wrong, black or white. Angel had a point, there's too many shades, too many damn shadows.

Yeah it's all fucked up, all of it and I'd had enough. Instinct and desire, it was the only way forward in the given situation and now I'm the bad guy. 'Stop me,' I'd begged Sal as I throttled the life out of her, shaking her up too much, way too much.

'I killed her and for what Angel?'

'Trust yourself a little more Ed, I swear it will be okay.'

'It'll be okay, I swear to you.' Sal used to say that, it was one of her sayings.

'You're just like her, Angel.'

In the time of right and wrong, of clear boundaries and precise delineations, I can even remember believing that my parents were perfect, they were my heroes. Their beliefs were the only beliefs, you know like everything else was some-how wrong. Shit what a fucking disappointment it was to discover that they too made mistakes, that they were human and fallible.

'I thought we were talking about Sal.'

'Same difference.'

'Ed you're all me, me, me.'

Self-obsessed

I, I, I.

I had reached the limit, the morning she arrived back from Rob's.

The policewoman accompanied her inside the flat and made Sal a nice cup of tea, heaped with spoonfuls of sugar. Before she left, she advised Sal on the benefits of psy-chotherapy.

'How could you?' I snarled at her, shaking my head, repulsed by her presence.

She sniffed, the edges of her mouth twitching.

'You sad fuck, look at you Sal, you've totally lost it.'

Did she really expect me to pick up the pieces, again? Of the two of us, who then would be the more pathetic?

'You've gone too far Sal.'

'I'm cracking up,' she stuttered, snivelling.

'Loser.'

'I'll ... I'll ... get it together, I swear.' She was gulping down her own words.

'It's over Sal.'

'No, please Ed, please.'

Full of remorse and begging for mercy, she fell to her knees, her arms clasped around my legs.

I took her into the bedroom and put her to sleep for good. 'Exactly how?' Fischer asked.

Jesus Christ, she'd idolized the guy

'What?' I replied

'How did you kill her?'

'I told you.'

'And the body? What did you do with her body?'

The evening after the fight and the gallant Fischer had arrived back at his flat to find us where he had left us, sprawled out on his sofa, Angel and I having spent the day recuperating. He'd stopped off at KFC and brought in a bucketful of chicken wings, chips, burgers and a couple of bottles of Vodka. We ate in silence at his small round table.

'So,' he began, twisting open the cap on the bottle of vodka. 'Here we are.'

That was how the conversation took off, how Fischer and I came to be acquainted. The first bottle sank over the usual banal introductory stuff, background info, but by the time we were on the second bottle, we had begun to trade life secrets.

'My lady did me over,' Fischer confessed.

'Snap, but in reverse,' I answered.

'She screwed my head you know.'

'Mine screwed her ex, and boss.'

'My best friend, Sasha,' spat out Fischer, refilling our small tumblers.

In a nutshell, Fischer's wife had left him for his best friend with the kid in tow. The boy he'd raised as his own and believed to be his son, but was revealed after seven years to have been spawned from another. This confession blurted out by his ex-wife, following one of their many acrimonious rows. The bitterest of blows winding him, devastated by the realization that the life he'd been living was a total sham. How catastrophic was that? Well, enough for Fischer to sell up everything he had, come over to Britain and work as a mini-cab driver in the hope of taking conversion exams which would (with any luck) allow him to practise as a doctor.

Fuelled on forty per cent proof, venting our hatred and disappointment with the cards we'd been dealt.

'Sal, she could have had anything.'

'I thought I had everything.'

Blind, the pair of us, our visions blurring as the second bottle emptied.

"So what did you do?

'What do you mean?'

'With her body?'

'Oh that.'

Disposing of the body was easy, I took the eco view, did my bit for the environment and went for the recycling option. What gets me though is the fact that everything now has a stunted lifespan. Why doesn't anything last, to be rendered obsolete so quickly, goddamn it, they have the friggin technology. Why, for example, can't the weekend papers sell in sections for like ten pence a section, so you don't have to carry around the sports and money pages that you ain't going to read anyhow.

I buried Sal, forcing her down, way down, she was all broken up, it was easy. Enough self-debasement for a lifetime, crumbling like flaky pastry, it was merely a matter of perspective. I relayed all this to Fischer.

'I took control, by God you can have whatever you desire and that's the footing I started off on. Instinct and Desire and fuck all that emotional baggage, that was Sal's deal.'

'I'm lonely, you stay with me,' slurred Fischer.

'Sure.' Besides there was nowhere else to go.

So Angel and I decided to stay put with Fischer for a few days, till her swelling subsided.

I pull the van over, right outside Rob's. Belsize Grove, and I haven't been along this way in a lifetime, an age. The large, white fronted house has a Sold sign displayed outside: so Rob really is moving out. Him and his wifey to be, getting something bigger. Well, well, perhaps they're planning on having a family, aw shucks and here we are about to fuck it all up.

'We're here. That's his flat.' I point to Rob's window, the curtains drawn, half smiling, adrenalin rushing, best high of all.

I laugh out loud, 'So . . . we've made it,' announcing the obvious. We have made it. Angel, Fischer and me, after a long hard night sitting in some stranger's van, outside Rob's.

'Feels weird, Angel doesn't it feel spooky?'

'Are you sure I look okay?'

'Yes, very lovely,' Fischer remarks. 'And the dress is good.'

'Okay Fischer, you know the score.'

'I'll wait for the signal.' The plan is finally about to be put into action. The signal was originally to have been a flashing torch, but as daylight is upon us, a wave from the window will suffice.

'I'll wave okay.'

'You wave and I'll come.'

'Yeah, I'll wave.'

'Ed, you nervous?' asks Angel. I am, but more nervous excited.

'Okay Angel, you ready?'

'Check.'

'You got everything?'

'Check.'

'Angel, if you say check again I'll clobber you.'

'Affirmative.' Jesus why can't she just be serious?

'We don't want to blow anything now.'

'Roger,' and she bit her tongue on the word. Roger the cunt, Coleen's henchman. He'd beat her up, took his fists to her bam . . . bam . . . bam with a little help from Neville of course. Christ but he had brutally laid into her, with all his force. Poor Angel she hadn't deserved that. I can hear her hissing under her breath, 'Check, check, and double bloody check, Ed.'

'Okay let's go.'

I swing open the car door and jump down to the pavement. Spinning round I meet Fischer's gaze and signal towards Ahmed.

'Fischer, if sleazeball should awaken, you think you can manage him?'

'He'll be out cold for the next hour at least.'

'Fischer . . .'

'What Edwards?'

'Here goes . . .'

'So go . . .'

'Okay . . . Fischer?'

'Good luck Edwards.'

I turn away from the car, reaching deep into my pocket for the keys to Rob's flat, up the six short steps to the front door.

'Angel, it's going to happen, I mean you're up for it, aren't you? You're not going to suddenly back down. Are you?'

'Am I Ed?' she asks sarcastically. 'Come on, let's get it over with.'

All the talk, mouthing off about what I'd do to Rob and here we are mounting the stairs, two by two, to the top landing, to Rob's door and my hands are shaky as I ease the keys into the latch and quietly turn the lock. The door opens and in we sneak.

Rob is a heavy sleeper, always has been, had relied on Sal rousing him. We sneak inside, the apartment full of light. The best thing about his place is the light, it's one of the brightest London flats I've ever been in. All around us stuff is strewn haphazardly, the place in chaotic disarray, as if Rob has thrown a wild party mere hours ago and we've arrived too late.

'Good timing Angel, hey imagine if things had gone to plan, it would never have worked.'

Bottles, cans, ashtrays overflowing, takeout cartons, slopped over the coffee-table, unopened wedding gifts from Harvey Nichols piled high. A groom's wedding suit hangs on the living room door, draped in plastic, a banner stuck to the mirror over the mantelpiece, HE'S GETTING MARRIED IN THE MORNING.

'Jesus Angel, look at the state of this room.'

Rob is usually obsessed by tidiness, too bad he never thought to clean up his own personal life but there you have it, the complexities of the human spirit.

A long time ago, when Sal was thick in love, she lost her heart over a dirty bastard dog. Yelped pitilessly when Rob announced he no longer loved her, well he loved her, but wasn't in love with her. Sal failed to understand the difference. He pointed out, that they, the two of them, the relationship wasn't going anywhere.

'Where do you want it to go?' she had pleaded.

'Don't make this more difficult than it already is.'

'I love you.'

'Sal, it's over.'

'Love just doesn't dry up and disappear, it just doesn't go, you can't fall in and out of it, we were meant to be together Rob, you and I . . . we have to be together.'

Begging for a second chance, Sal scratched at his door, refusing to give up on him. Christ this occurred so long ago and you'd have thought she'd have gotten over it by now. Why the fuck are we standing in Rob's hallway at 7.30 on a Thursday morning, it doesn't feel right anymore?

'Ed, I think I'd rather go to Barcelona than Paris,' Angel whispers over to me.

'Yeah, the weather might be better.'

We creep towards the bedroom, the door slightly ajar, the floorboards creaking as we make our way in. My hand leans heavily on the handle and pushes aside the door . . .

The plan. The point of it all.

It had come to me by chance while walking up Stroud Green Road with a massive hangover from the vodka consumed on my second night in Fischer's. I was on a paranoid downer, you know when you wake up and all you can hear are those grey-matter demons raging. Every substance consumed over the past few weeks was struggling out of my system. My head throbbed, I was uncomfortable in my own skin, and to top it all, it was freezing. The only way to deal with my condition was to try and walk it off.

Angel and I staggered out into the blustery morning and made our way over to Finsbury Park, over the bridge, past the tennis courts to the artificial lake. The place was fairly desolate, a few straggling old gents and dog owners, unleashing their pets so they could have a crap on the common. Angel tugged along at my side. I wasn't convinced by her presence, felt she may be a burden, a weight I'd have to carry and instinctively she kept her mouth shut as we did the circuit around the lake. My ears stung from the cold, fingers rigid and those demons kept on with their whinging insistence, fuelling my head with hatred and resentment towards every living thing but mostly myself. Then her voice started at me, oftentimes I'd hear Sal's voice, it would echo through me.

Words from beyond, Sal's voice resonating in my head: 'Ed, it's cold in here. Ed, where are you? Ed? Ed?' Wistful, barely audible, seeping through me: 'Ed, I don't like this game. I'm sorry Ed, okay you win, please Ed? It's freezing in here.'

'Go away,' I snarled, in no mood to listen to some harpy.

'Ed, it's cold, it's over okay? We'll call it quits. I want to come out. Come and get me, I'm tired of this. Ed please?'

'Shut up Sal, you're dead. Corpses don't speak.'

'I'm sorry. Ed . . .'

And I'm telling myself to snap out of it, that Sal doesn't

exist and it's just a head hoax but she seemed so lost in herself.

'Ed, I swear I'm sorry. I was all wrong, please, you got to believe me Ed. It's over, you win. Come and get me Ed? I've learnt my lesson.'

This wasn't about any lesson, how could she think it was some kind of punishment, that wasn't the reason things came to an end, you got to move on, let go.

'Listen Sal there's this story about two brothers.'

'Ed, stop, will you let me out. I'm tired of this stupid game.'

'Willy!' a little lady stooped over by age scuttled past Angel and myself, hollering, 'Willy,' her voice shrill and insistent, 'Willy!'

She'd lost her Willy; it's a wonder how dog owners go about choosing pet names. She was Ethel out of *EastEnders*, before the pair of them died.

Jump for me Pavlov

'Angel, look it's Ethel out of *EastEnders*.'

Sal used to watch *EastEnders* religiously during her teens, in the days when Den was dirty and Angie tottered on the edge but she rapidly went off it at precisely the moment Den was revealed to be the father of Michelle Fowler's illegitimate kid. Now there was a surname to suit the person, you couldn't get a fouler-looking teenager than Michelle, her plain face scarred with acne. Sal just didn't buy it, that Den would have shagged Miss Fowler. Den wasn't half bad looking in the rough and ready sort of way, could have screwed anyone on the square. It didn't add up, so Sal swapped allegiance and switched over to *Brookside*.

The Ethel look-a-like continued calling out for her Willy. She peered over at us, as if about to ask for some helpful intervention but shrank back, most probably put off by the state of Angel. Poor love, must have been scared by our crude presence. I let my head hang low and made off in the opposite direction, just as Willy jumped out of the far bushes and came bounding over to his owner with a mangy half a bird hanging from his jaws.

'Good boy, there's a good boy,' relieved to have her bull terrier back and she patted him while putting on the lead, the bird remains dropped at her feet, she kicked them aside, then tootled off.

'We should go Angel,' I muttered, my stomach queasy, in need of carbo-refreshment.

Angel didn't bother to reply and we exited the park and began our trawl up Stroud Green Road. Stumbling onward, eyes directed to the ground, avoiding contact with passersby, because we kept encountering glares, like I had two heads. This was our first public outing since the fight and if she got one more pitying glance, she'd have crumbled.

I was in no mood to be the point of focus in one of those trendy cafés that play hip world music and serve fat chips. You know the type of establishment, with pretty young waitresses, all skinny and studenty, serving you up huge portions of sweet cake, where everyone is vying everyone else or chatting merrily about how well their lives are going. Where have all the shitty places gone, the greasy, soulless caffs of yesteryear. We'd trudged up the hill to Crouch End, our search fruitless, our stomachs howling and then decided to turn back.

Those damn demons on at me for having wasted so much time these past weeks, when I should have dealt with Rob, formulated a plan worthy of this feeling of vengeance that was gnawing at my conscience.

On the downward slope, we passed Ethel again, Willy was sniffing at the butt of a mongrel bitch, whose owner attempted to tug her dog free.

'He's a one,' joked Ethel.

Angel and I stopped at a Chippies, at last a perfect dive for our purpose, glaring light and plastic furniture (the sort usually found outside caravans, white, light and cheap). I bought a couple of portions of mushy peas and chips, and a couple of cans of Coke. Jacked up on carbo and sugar and pretty soon I was feeling okay.

'You want more chips?'

'Sure,' replied Angel. So up I went again and once more Willy appeared within my realm of vision, this time rubbing up against a human leg, clad in denim.

'Angel it's just occurred.'

'What?'

'I was thinking about Rob. He's a dog.'

'What do you mean?'

'Dog, bow wow.'

In the worst sense of the word, always on the sniff, prowl, any hole would do. I'd said it before, this canine allusion, without realizing exactly what I meant, failing to listen to myself. I popped open the second can and that's when it came to me.

See I'd made a mistake, got hung up by my own hatred, my desire to wipe Rob out without resorting to murder. To destroy someone, break them down, like Rob had done to Sal, to dismantle them slowly, but in my case the aim was to do the deed in one swipe. This was the point where my imagination stalled and fizzled. I couldn't quite make the mental jump. Yet all the time it was staring me in the face. Rob, well you know, he had an eye for the ladies, dick for brains; you see, there was no way to sever the link between the eye, and prick without physically blinding him. Rob was the one I wanted to teach a lesson to, to punish, avenge for the way he had discarded Sal, for his attitude to her sex. I wanted to deflate him so that he would learn something, cast him from his position of power. Highlight the difference between us. That was it, I'd hit the nail on the head. Me, I could never satisfy Sal, I'd not the physical capacity to fulfil her, that was beyond our dimension. My impotency.

See, the point of it all was to have Rob feel how I felt, wear my shoes. Was it possible that I could, for just a while, for a brief period of time, have Rob taste the reality which was my own? His monumental potency undone.

'What do you think Angel?'

'I dunno, I mean . . . it sounds complicated.'

'How complicated can it be?' Those mutts and moggies, done over, for their own good, spayed, cut, desexed, impotent, rendered useless.

'So you're suggesting we cut off Rob's balls?'

Metaphorically ... yes. That was exactly what I was proposing. But there had to be another way, a cleaner, more sanitized way, in which one could attain this ideal.

'Fischer, he's a doctor, he'll know.'

'Yeah but he's a guy and you know how protective they are of their manhood's.'

To the point of religious obsession. All hail the dick. I'd offer to pay him.

'Hey Angel, don't forget we got the money. Frank's money, may as well put it to good use.'

Plain sailing after that little bout of inspiration and Angel and I became immersed in the practicalities of how to convince Fischer to come in with us.

'Fischer, know anything about impotency?' After all, I myself could tell him a thing or two.

When we arrived back, laden down with bags of shopping and bottles of spirit, Fischer was writing in one of his many notebooks.

'Edwards, feel any better?'

'Yeah a lot.'

'Fischer, if you could get back at Sasha for screwing your wife, what would you do?'

'Do?' He paused for like all of a nano second. 'I'd break his balls.'

And so ... I tried to explain my desire for vengeance. Slowly it had taken precedence over everything and I, enslaved by it, yearned only to be released from its grip. This,

I disclosed to Fischer, was my sole pursuit, at last I felt within reach of an answer. Anaesthetizing the dog, could it be done, without surgically denying the guy of his manhood, or physically maiming him?

'Is it possible?'

'Everything is possible.' I liked Fischer's attitude.

'To put the dick to sleep, do you see what I'm getting at?'

'Edwards, what you ask is unethical, it is . . .'

'A just retribution. An apt punishment. I'm not asking for the world and . . . I'd pay you.'

'How much?'

'Enough. We're talking thousands. Interested?'

'Let me think about it.'

I left Fischer to ponder on the possibility and took the bus to Kentish Town to pay Neville a final visit and I hadn't seen him since the night of the fight.

'Neville, you complete bastard.' I marched into his flat and threw him back the spare set of keys he'd lent me.

'Ed, what you doing here?' My presence shocked him and he jumped up out of the chair and started backing towards the wall.

'Listen it was all Roger's fault, he told me he'd kill me . . .'

'I don't want to hear.' I pushed Neville back down into the chair. 'You complete shit.'

'Listen Ed, I swear to you . . . Roger had me, he . . .'

'Neville, you're going to have to make this up to me.'

'Ed . . . whatever you want, some grass, pills, what?'

One night, a fair while back, during the good old days, Neville had imparted a nugget of information that I thought may be of use, in my present circumstances.

'Neville, the gun.'

'Ed don't kill me, please . . . I'm begging you . . . please.'

'Where's the gun?'

'Ed, I swear, I tried to tell you.' In the meantime, I tied Neville to the chair so he wouldn't try to make a run for it. Shit scared he was.

'Jesus H. Just tell me where the gun is?'

He complied and I got it.

'Where's Roger?'

'They've gone.'

'What?'

'They've gone back to Scotland.'

'You telling me the truth?'

'Ed, man, cross my heart, they left earlier today.'

'Lucky for them. Neville, you really disappointed me. I mean, Christ, look at the state of me. I'm totally fucked.'

'I'm sorry Ed.'

'Yeah? I'm sorry too,' and I truly was, 'cause Neville's basically a good guy albeit a retard.

'Look take care of yourself Nev and stay out of trouble.'

I left him tied to the chair, his effort to escape would give him something to occupy himself with for the next few hours. Then I headed back to Fischer's.

The gun was for emergency use only, should Rob get a bit difficult, if he put up a struggle, I thought it would have a calming affect.

'So Fischer, can I count you in?'

'There is a way, I'll have to get my hands on some drugs but yes, Edwards, it's possible, we may be able to come to an agreement.'

Where was Angel in all this?

Hovering in the background awaiting instructions. My

sweet little honeypot, the plan dependent on her compli-
ance in carrying out the practicalities of the operation.

In my mind's eye it came into focus something along
the lines of this. We'd arrive at Rob's, steal into his apartment, creep into his room and then Angel would get down
on her knees and pray that what we had in mind would
work.

It hinged on the knowledge of one of Rob's fantasies,
the one where he wakes to find a beautiful stranger sucking him off. Yeah, whatever turns you on. His whimsy
elaborating into a minor S&M scenario whereupon sight of
this bewitching woman, an Angel in disguise, she would
then commence to tie him to the bed and have her wicked
way. On occasion it may be acknowledged, Sal had indeed
played out the role. Anyhow, in the present circumstances
and given the fact Rob was to be married later in the day,
the plan seemed perfect in every conceivable way. Hence
Angel was to pleasure Rob, while I took to tying him
down. A signal would then alert Fischer and he would
come up to finish off the job, insert the needle and release
the venom.

So we arrived at Rob's, later than planned, but we got
there in the end and entered his apartment, the place was in
a state, crap strewn all over, the door to his bedroom slightly
ajar, Angel was distracting herself with thoughts of travel
and we crept inside his room and . . .

Back to the car.

'Aw Jesus . . .' My eyes scrunched tight, my hands over
my face.

'You okay?' Fischer still sitting in the passenger seat, per-
plexed to see me.

'No, yeah, I don't know.' Biting my thumbnail, 'Shit Fischer.'

'What happened?'

'He wasn't there.'

'What?'

'Rob wasn't there.'

'What?'

'The place was empty.'

'You say he was going to be there.'

'I assumed he would be.'

'Excuse me?'

Have I really planned this whole scenario on the mere assumption that Rob would be home?

'Edwards, that's not like you.'

I wonder if Fischer reckons I've backed out of it at the last moment, that my nerve has quit on me, maybe he'd half expected this to happen all along. Maybe he'd hoped I'd back down. So I'd rush back to the car with a flimsy excuse, claiming Rob wasn't there.

Of course he was there, sprawled on the bed, naked, the covers tossed aside. The floorboards creaking as Angel and I stole into his bedroom.

'Justine?' he'd murmured, deep in sleep.

Several moments lapsed as I'd gaped at Rob, prostrate, lying there in total vulnerability, almost Godlike.

A chink of light through the curtains fell on his bedside table, a white medicinal box of sleeping tablets. Instinctively, I reached out to pocket them. You never know when they could come in handy.

I noticed three alarm clocks, wedding presents? Who cares, but they were all set for 10. First thing I did was unset them. Poor Rob must have had a rough night, taken a couple of sleeping pills 'cause when Angel prodded him there was zero reaction.

I'd rushed back to the car. 'Shit I need a fag.' I really needed a smoke.

'Course he's there, splat out, dead to the world, I mean there was no need to . . . you know . . .'

'So you don't give up?'

You know, somewhere in the depths of my consciousness, I'd half expected to find Rob already undone, as if there was a natural justice in the world and the wedding had been called off and he'd have woken up to find me in his flat.

Teasing myself, I'd played out the scenario in my head a dozen times, something along these lines:

'Justine . . .?' Rob mumbles, turning his body on the bed.

'Justine, is that you babe?' Rob's eyes blinking open in the half light of the morning.

'I love you Justine . . . I,' Rob's tone beseeching.

'It's not Justine.' The sound of my voice distant like some phantom.

I answer Rob and he screws up his eyes, as if unsure he's asleep or not.

'Justine? Baby is that you?'

'It's me, Rob.'

'You?'

Surprise, surprise, like some recurring nightmare.

Instinctively he pulls the covers over his nakedness and looks at me like I have a gun in my hand. Actually I'd forgotten, I would have the gun in my hand, lowering it . . .

'What the hell? What are you doing here?'

'Thought I'd call by, wish you good luck for later today.' (How corny was that!)

'It's off,' he replies flatly.

Come again and I'm veritably shocked.

'What do you mean it's off?'

He switches on the bedside lamp.

'What's happened to you?'

'Had a bit of a run-in with someone.'

'Are you okay?'

'Getting there.'

'She dumped me. She's left me.'

'Maybe it's for the best.'

'What?' His drowsy confusion overwhelming and scratching his head dumbfounded, he asks me again, 'What are you doing here?'

'I'm going away, properly I mean, I'm leaving the country, thought I'd say goodbye, wish you good luck with the wedding.'

'It's off.'

'Yeah you said.'

Justine has found out he was sleeping around and left.

'Sorry to hear that, thought you two made a lovely couple.'

Rob starts appealing to my better judgement, to stray pangs of compassion.

'I've fucked things up so bad ... It's too late now ... it's over ... ruined. Christ I'm sorry.'

All neat and tidy and ultimately cowardly.

Yesterday I was so certain of how events would unfold, it was all worked out in my head. I woke late, booked a couple of seats on Eurostar, first class, to start as I meant to go on, then tubed it into Charing Cross to pick up my bag with the money. I called Fischer, arranged to meet him later, caught an afternoon movie, a soft romance that would appeal to the masses, guaranteed to be a huge commercial success, bummed around the bookshops, then had something to eat. Restless I spent the whole time rehearsing what would happen later on. Nothing had gone as planned, everything stacked up against me, impediments piled high and over I'd stumbled, face down in the muck and now at the last hurdle was I to shirk it?

Without Sal, I'd tasted an uncontrolled freedom, there were no moral boundaries to my behaviour. I was having fun, no repercussions to thwart me, no time for analytical digressions, doing just as I pleased, whatever that entailed, until the day my moral conscience smacked into me. My guardian angel swooped down from high, I'd taken such a beating and she said, 'It'll be okay, I swear to you, it will work out fine.'

By now you know me pretty well, you keeping up? The picture coming into focus? Reader (yes, you, and I think at this stage I can address you directly), well, I'm not going to spell it out, I refuse to insult your intelligence.

I knew Rob would be there 'cause I had phoned him yesterday. This was the gist of how the conversation went.

'Hi Rob.'

'*You*, what are *you* calling for?' He was not pleased to hear from me. Amidst his ranting and calling me everything under the sun, I managed to squeak out the following.

'I wanted to wish you luck for the wedding.'

'You fucking . . . do you have any idea how much trouble you've caused?'

'Me?'

'Don't play dumb, you're dead bitch.' Beat you to it.

'Mmm okay . . . well have a nice life.' But he'd already slammed down the receiver.

Dead air. My girl Sal, the cause of so much mayhem, so, even at her most pathetic she'd managed to achieve something. I had needed to hear his voice to confirm my own hatred, to give me the extra little push required. Hey, he deserved a wedding present, besides it's not every day you get married.

At this juncture and if I'm honest, the moment I walked back into that flat, I knew in my heart it was over. Rob's hold on me had evaporated, our common scent dispersed, our history completed. I no longer recognized the ties that had bound us, like the scene in the afternoon movie when an ex-lover merged back into the crowd and disappeared for good. I was smoking on a Marlboro Light, edging towards the icing on the cake.

I stamp out the half-smoked cigarette, Fischer is already standing on the pavement, tying a knot in his dressing gown belt.

'Come on Angel.'

I take a deep, deep, breath.

Up we go, back to the flat to finish the job off properly.

Personally I can vouch for Fischer's deftness of touch, a simple injection was to do the trick. Fischer had offered me a choice between a botox injection into the nerves or an oestrogen one, both rendering a limp dick for a month at most. The latter choice was easier to obtain and I got Fischer to write out a false prescription for the amount required and handed it over the counter. The pharmacist had raised her eyes at me and rang Fischer directly. The cow didn't buy it 'cause I so didn't look like a tranny. In the end, I had to trawl round various chemists asking for the morning-after pill.

Since the age of twelve I've had that cursed oestrogen raging through me, causing all sorts of mayhem, making me grow tits, stunting my nub so that's it's within an inch of itself, if that (before you ask, size does matter), softening me up, making me weak, moody, bleeding me dry. Once, twice, three times a lady.

We stand at the edge of Rob's bed, Fischer has liquefied the pills and has the needle ready. Pre-prepared he presses the end and out squirts a drop of the substance. Rob's ass exposed and I lean over him, pinning him to the bed. The final thrust, down it plunges, piercing his flesh. Fischer emptying the syringe into Rob's system to the last drop. On impact Rob wakes into a slumbered state of shock; I practically bounce off him, he slumps back down and we flee. The guy won't know what hit him. The whole process takes less than five minutes.

And that's it.

Fischer and I run back to the car.

'Man this thing is driving me crazy.' I pull Imelda's blasted wig off my scalp.

Yeah, I'm feeling much more centred now, more like my old self.

'Fischer, thanks.'

'For what, Angel? I did not do much.'

'Yeah you did.'

I press the key in the ignition.

'You know I'm glad we met.'

'Me also Miss Edwards.'

'We gotta dump the car and sleazeball back at St Mary's.'

'Okay.'

Fischer has these intense eyes, black lashed and when he

looks at me, I get this nervy feeling in the pit of my stomach and my cheeks redden.

I give him a sideways glance.

'You know, I was thinking, Barcelona may be nicer than Paris this time of year.'

'But there's certain romance with Paris, you think?'

'Boris, are you . . .?'

'What Sal?'

Hey and already we were on first-name terms.

'Nothing, it doesn't matter.'

Wash me I'm Filthy

GUILDFORD LIBRARY

www.surreycc.gov.uk/libraries

Overdue items may incur charges
as published in the current
Schedule of Charges.

SURREY
COUNTY COUNCIL

L21